DEAD CENTRE

Recent Titles by Claire Lorrimer from Severn House

Inspector Govern and Sergeant Beck Mysteries

OVER MY DEAD BODY

DEAD CENTRE

BENEATH THE SUN

CONNIE'S DAUGHTER

DECEPTION

THE FAITHFUL HEART

FOR ALWAYS

NEVER SAY GOODBYE

AN OPEN DOOR

THE RECKONING

THE RELENTLESS STORM

THE REUNION

THE SEARCH FOR LOVE

SECOND CHANCE

SECRET OF QUARRY HOUSE

THE SHADOW FALLS

TROUBLED WATERS

A VOICE IN THE DARK

THE WOVEN THREAD

DEAD CENTRE

Claire Lorrimer

This first world edition published in Great Britain 2005 by
SEVERN HOUSE PUBLISHERS LTD of
9–15 High Street, Sutton, Surrey SM1 1DF.
This first world edition published in the USA 2005 by
SEVERN HOUSE PUBLISHERS INC of
595 Madison Avenue, New York, N.Y. 10022.

British Library Cataloguing in Publication Data

Lorrimer,   Claire
   Dead centre
   1.   Police - Great Britain - Fiction
   2.   Detective and mystery stories
   I.   Title
   823.9'14 [F]

   ISBN 0-7278-6203-0

Typeset by Palimpsest Book Production Ltd.,
Polmont, Stirlingshire, Scotland.
Printed and bound in Great Britain by
MPG Books Ltd., Bodmin, Cornwall.

For Mel, who taught me how to play golf
and who has been my loving partner ever since

One

It started to rain, the clouds obscuring the moonlight so that Poppy was now guided only by the glow of the solar lamps spaced at intervals along the path. When she reached the spinney to the left of the path, a gust of wind sent the branches of a rowan tree swinging across her face. She put up her arm to protect herself, but too late to avoid a blow across the back of her shoulders, knocking her off balance. Hitting the wet ground, she felt a swift stab of fear as she realized it was no branch but the heavy weight of a man's body now falling on top of her.

She opened her mouth to scream but her assailant's hand quickly covered her mouth.

'Shut up and I won't hurt you!' The voice was a hoarse whisper. She thought it was familiar but she couldn't identify the owner. It was an educated accent and although most of the breath had left her lungs when she hit the ground, she managed to jerk her head sideways and gasp, 'Please, let me go! I won't scream, I promise. Please!'

There was no reply but now she felt her arms being twisted behind her and what she took to be a belt fastening her wrists together. She knew then that, whoever the man was, he intended either to rape or kill her, and she started to struggle. He turned her over on her back and she tried to kick out at him but the weight of his body made movement of any kind impossible.

Suddenly, without warning, the cloud that had covered the moon moved away and Poppy saw the man's face. With a shock, she recognized the elderly golf club member with whom she had been dancing earlier.

1

'Gordon!' she gasped. 'Please, Mr Rivers . . . Gordon . . . let me go!'

Even as she spoke she knew it was pointless to do so. His breath reeked of alcohol, his face was suffused with colour, and as he straddled her she was no longer in doubt as to his intention. He was going to rape her.

'You deserve this!' he panted as with one hand he pulled up her skirt. 'You and that twin sister of yours ask for it, don't you, exposing your bellies, tossing your heads and flirting with those gormless boys. The pair of you have been asking for it . . . and I'm going to give it to you . . .'

He prised open her legs with his knee, still using the upper part of his body to prevent her retaliating. His face came close to hers. His breath was hot on her cheek as she tried to turn aside.

'Don't pretend you don't want it!' he hissed. 'You're all the same, you women, flaunting yourselves, asking for it. I'm going to—'

They were the last words Gordon Rivers ever spoke. The weight of a golf club struck him with considerable force on the back of his head. His body sank on top of Poppy's.

Twisting her head frantically to one side Poppy saw her identical twin sister, Rose, staring down at her, the club still in her hand.

'Get him off me! Get him off!' Poppy shouted hysterically. 'Get him off me, please!'

Rose had heard the man's voice before she saw him; heard his threats and run forward. She then saw the two figures, the man's body on top of her sister. Beside their feet, clearly visible in the moonlight, was the golf club which, unbeknown to Rose, Poppy had used as a makeshift crutch and dropped when she was attacked. Hearing the noise of Rose's approach, Rivers had turned, and without hesitation Rose had picked up the club and swung it with all her strength against his head.

His body twitched and, afraid he was about to move, Rose struck him again, this time missing his head and hitting him across the shoulders.

Poppy now struggled out from beneath him. Rose undid the belt round Poppy's wrists and they clung to one another, sobbing hysterically. After several minutes Rose calmed down sufficiently to whisper, 'I don't think he's moving, Poppy. I may have killed him.'

'Don't touch him! Don't!' Poppy pleaded as Rose bent down and, rolling Rivers over on to his back, felt the pulse in his neck.

'Why, it's Gordon Rivers!' she whispered. 'He's dead, Pops. And I don't care. He was going to rape you!'

Unable to speak, Poppy merely nodded. She was still too terrified to think clearly, but Rose was now fully alert.

'The boys will have guessed by now that I came to find you and they will be looking for us. I've got to stop them coming here.'

Poppy and Rose were strikingly pretty girls with their father's Irish colouring, dark hair and violet blue eyes. Not only were they pretty with tall, slim figures, but the twins were fourteen and thirteen handicap golfers, good tennis players and much in demand by the other first-year students at Sussex University, where they studied.

Earlier that evening Poppy had tripped over someone's golf bag in the locker room of the Cheyne Manor Golf Club where a party was in progress to celebrate the tenth year of its inception. Poppy had been dancing with her current boyfriend, Fred, and he had looked at her with some concern when she told him she had twisted her ankle and would like to return to her room in the nearby Cheyne Manor Hotel, take a painkiller and go to bed.

Not wanting her twin to leave the disco in sympathy, she'd refused Fred's offer to drive her and, unaware that she was being followed, she had taken the footpath, which was only three hundred yards across the golf course.

Rose now drew her mobile from her jacket pocket and called her boyfriend, John McNaught.

John, a tall, fair-haired American, was in the entrance way regarding the worried expression on his friend Fred's face.

Shorter by nearly half a metre, Fred Clark decided that although he had promised Poppy not to tell her twin she'd left the party, there would be no harm in telling John now that Rose, too, had departed.

'Pops twisted her ankle and, as it was hurting, she decided to go home,' he said. 'You and Rose were snogging on the dance floor and she made me promise not to tell Rose she'd left as she knew Rose would leave the party and go after her.'

John stared at Fred's bespectacled face, partly in relief now he was pretty sure he knew where Rose was, but also in some annoyance.

'Even if you didn't tell Rose about Poppy, you should have told me,' he said. 'Poppy didn't walk, I take it? You drove her back to the hotel?'

The twins had a grace-and-favour apartment at Cheyne Manor, which had once been their family home. Their father, Julian Matheson, had been unable to find the money to pay the exhorbitant inheritance tax levied on the estate when his father died, and, being unable to get planning permission to develop the land for housing, had sold it and moved his family to the south of France. When his identical twin daughters had opted to go back to England and to read Sociology at Sussex University, he had negotiated a lengthy lease on the attic rooms in the Manor, which he had paid to have converted into a delightful three-room apartment.

Fred returned John's gaze uneasily.

'I wanted to drive her but she wouldn't let me. You know what those girls are like, John. Poppy got it into her head that if Rose saw me around the place, she'd suppose Poppy was with me and at least enjoy herself for a while longer.'

'She *walked* back – with a bad ankle?' John queried. 'That sounds real crazy!'

'I said so, too,' Fred agreed. 'But, as Poppy said, the short cut across the golf course to the hotel only takes five minutes at most – and that path is lit, as you know.' He paused before adding: 'She took her driver as a sort of crutch. I'm sure she'll be all right.'

Nevertheless, John considered that golf courses were not the safest place to be at night and the short cut to the hotel was likely to be deserted. Granted it was only a short distance running the length of the 18th fairway, but there were trees and shrubs on either side where it neared the boundary wall of the hotel garden.

'Despite what you say, I'm worried, Fred!' he said. 'Those two girls are so alike they even seem to share the same thoughts, and about ten minutes ago Rose and I were having a drink when she suddenly stood up and went rushing out of the room without a single word. I supposed she'd been caught short, and, after a minute or two, I went round to the changing rooms to see if she was okay. That's when that creep Armitage told me he'd seen her dashing out through the front door. I'm sure something's wrong, Fred. I'm going to telephone the hotel. There's bound to be someone about.'

There was, however, no need to do so. As he was reaching for his mobile phone it rang. Despite the noise coming from the dance floor, he could hear Rose's voice quite clearly.

'They're safely back at the hotel,' he mouthed to Fred. 'Poppy's fine.' He turned back to his mobile. 'Love you, honey!' he said, his tone casual because he knew Rose was not ready yet for any kind of commitment. Together with her identical twin they were thoroughly enjoying university life. They'd become a foursome of friends, playing golf, and tennis whenever they wished on the hotel hard court. All four had been pretty inseparable since their arrival at the university the previous October, parting only during the Christmas vacation when the girls had gone back to France to their parents and John went to stay in Glasgow with Fred.

'You had me worried for a bit,' Fred said as they went back to the bar. 'But you know how stubborn Pops can be and she really didn't want me with her.'

As Fred was voicing his concern, Poppy was saying almost the same words to Rose.

'I wish I'd let Fred come with me – he wanted to!' she said. 'Perhaps I should have been more wary of . . . of Mr Rivers!'

5

Both girls stared down at the body. The breeze was blowing his wispy grey hair and they were momentarily terrified lest he had moved.

'He has . . . had . . .' Rose corrected herself with a shiver '. . . a horrible way of staring at you! But I never imagined . . . not rape! Oh, Pops, I can't bear to think what it must have been like for you . . .'

Both were shivering as they turned once more to stare at the body.

'What are we going to do, Rose?' Poppy whispered. 'We can't just leave him here. Someone may come along and . . . Fred knew I was taking the short cut . . .'

Her voice trailed into silence as Rose said in a voice that trembled despite her attempt to remain calm: 'You didn't kill him, Pops. I did!'

'But if I say *I* did, it would be self-defence,' Poppy said quickly, adding almost inaudibly, '. . . not murder!'

Rose bit her lip, unaware of the rain now falling on them both – and on the body.

'We'll have to move him somewhere – we can drag him . . . over there by the wall.'

Poppy followed Rose's pointing finger.

'He'd be seen there in daylight . . .' she said doubtfully. 'If we could get him over the wall, Rose, into the hotel shrubbery. They might not find him there for ages and then they'd suspect someone in the hotel had killed him.'

Rose nodded. Both she and Poppy were reluctant to touch the dead man, but, knowing it was dangerous to leave him lying there, they finally did so. Surprisingly, there was no blood coming from the back of his head where the golf club had hit him. They replaced his belt and, with Rose at his feet and Poppy supporting his shoulders, they struggled with great difficulty to carry him towards the dry stone wall. Both were breathing hard as finally they managed to heave his body over the wall where it disappeared into a heavy growth of rhododendron and azalea bushes.

'Rose – my golf club – its still lying there . . .' Poppy whispered.

'I'll get it,' Rose said. Rejoining her twin, she noticed with a fresh stab of anxiety that they were both covered with mud.

'We'd better go in the staff entrance. There won't be anyone around at this time, and Miss Cahill doesn't do her lock-up round until midnight. We'd better hurry though – it's a quarter past eleven now.'

Fortunately for both girls, the servants' entrance and stair-case were deserted. Some of the staff had gone down to help at the club, and the kitchen staff had long since gone back to their homes in the nearby village of Ferrydene. It was not until the twins were back in their own sitting room, the door to their apartment locked, that they allowed themselves to consider their situation.

'Maybe we shouldn't have moved him,' Rose said thought-fully. 'Maybe we should have called the police.'

'But, Rose, it was *murder*!' Poppy whispered. 'They would arrest you, put you in prison, and if there was a trial . . .'

'There'd have to be, even if we both said we'd done it. I could pretend I was the one who Rivers attacked and you hit him and you'd say the same and then they couldn't prove which one and—'

'Rose, the club. It might have blood or something horrible on it. Thank God you brought it back with you.'

'We'd better hide it!' Rose said thoughtfully. 'We could put it down in the cellar with Papa's clubs. He won't be using them this Easter holiday, and when everything's blown over we can put it back in your bag. You can borrow his so no one notices yours has gone.'

'I feel sick!' Poppy said, leaning back in her armchair and drawing deep breaths. 'I don't think we can confess, Rose, even though we didn't mean him to die. Think what awful publicity there'd be – hordes of reporters all over the hotel and golf course and Fred and John would get involved and then there's Papa and Ma . . . they'd be devastated. Pa's last words were "I know I can trust you both to behave!" Rose, we can't tell the police. We can't tell anyone – ever!'

Rose remained silent, her eyes thoughtful as she regarded her sister. Then she said in a low, firm voice: 'I'm not sorry for what I did, Poppy. That man was going to rape you. I'm glad he's dead. He deserved to die if that's what he does to people. If I'm sorry about anything it's that one of us had to do it.'

Poppy jumped out of her chair and running across the room to her twin she put her arms round her and they clung to one another, weeping quietly.

And so they finally slept, clasped to each other, fearful of the nightmares that might beset them, and with visions of the dead man lying under the rhododendron bushes in the rain.

As the revellers left the clubhouse in jovial high spirits, not one of them realized April 3rd would be remembered in future not for the club's inception but for being the first of the Cheyne Manor Golf Club's murders.

Two

It was Deborah Cahill, the assistant manageress of Cheyne Manor Hotel, who found the body. As was her unbroken custom, she always took her beloved Yorkshire terrier for a last walk at night before locking up and retiring to bed. Even if it was pouring with rain, although she might shorten her walk, Deborah still kept to the routine that her dog expected. Tonight, because of the threatening rain, she took him only to the boundary of the hotel garden where it adjoined the golf course rather than making a circuit of the moderately extensive grounds. It was therefore exactly midnight on the Tuesday evening when she reached the boundary wall and Rusty's furious barking halted her in her tracks. Following the dog into the shrubbery, she was horrified to find Rusty pawing at the prone body of a man.

At the age of fifty-seven, unmarried and with no relatives or dependents, Deborah Cahill had become a disciplined and resourceful woman as well as an indispensable and highly efficient PA to Kevin Harris, the owner of Cheyne Manor Hotel and Golf Club. Now, despite her certainty that the man lying on his side half in and half out of the undergrowth was dead, she did not have hysterics as might other less confident females, but caught hold of Rusty's collar with one hand, and, tucking him under her arm, dragged the man's arm from beneath the bushes in order to feel for his pulse with the other. Although none was to be felt, she noticed that the body was still slightly warm despite the drizzle of rain which had curtailed her walk that evening.

The dead man's face was partly obscured by his damp grey

hair, which straggled across the pale cheeks, and by the horn-rimmed spectacles that had slipped down over his mouth; but as the initial shock began to lessen, Deborah realized who he was – one of their permanent guests who had a single room on the first floor of the hotel. A Scot by the name of Rivers, he had been living in England since his retirement. He kept himself very much to himself but was a fanatical golfer who spent most of his time on the course and only appeared in the hotel to sleep and for meals.

Standing up, Deborah peered across the night-darkened lawn and flower beds with the first feeling of fear. Was there someone still out there in the darkness, watching her perhaps? Of a certainty, unless a person like herself was walking a dog, they would not be walking for exercise or pleasure at this time of night and especially not distant from the gravelled paths. Unless the unfortunate Mr Rivers, at whose body Rusty was still furiously barking, had stumbled accidentally into the bushes and suffered a heart attack, some unknown person must have harmed him by unknown means.

She bent to look once more at the body. A sudden shaft of moonlight revealed a large swelling on the back of his head; so it was not a heart attack, she realized.

'Come along, Rusty,' she said sharply as she felt another frisson of fear. She attached his lead, which was always a necessity once she turned for "home" and he realized his walk was nearly over. 'We must go and find Mr Harris.'

Despite the three decades she had worked for Kevin Harris, first as a secretary in London and then as his PA when he bought and converted the rambling manor house and estate into a hotel and golf course, she had retained the formal employer-employee relationship. This was partly because she had fallen in love with him when she'd first met him and remained in love for the subsequent thirty years. The fact that he was married to a beautiful, voluptuous Spanish woman and that she, herself, was rather plain – tall, gawky and angular – precluded any possible hope that he might one day fall out of love with his wife and in love with her. She had contented

herself, therefore, with becoming totally indispensable to him
– someone he leaned on; someone he needed; someone in
whom he could confide his anguish at his wife's frequent infi-
delities and who could soothe him with her sensible advice,
not to mention her flattery and ability to restore his ego.

A self-made man, with very little education, Kevin Harris
relied upon Deborah to write his letters, correct his grammar,
offer advice when he had to deal with socially superior guests
and generally steer him in the right directions. Despite his
humble beginnings, he had an instinct for making money –
enough, by the time he was forty, to buy the eighteenth-
century Cheyne Manor estate down near the Sussex coast. The
property had been put up for sale when Sir Julian Matheson's
father had died and he had been unable to find the wherewithal to pay the death duties.

Kevin had been astute enough before he'd exchanged
contracts to make certain of planning permission to turn the
house into a hotel and the accompanying three hundred and
seventy-five acres into an excellent eighteen-hole golf course.
Golfers could now book package holidays, staying in the
extremely comfortable Cheyne Manor Hotel and able to walk
to the bottom of the garden to watch the players on the fifth
green.

From a gate in the boundary wall, a path led directly past
the eighteenth fairway to the clubhouse, thus avoiding quite
a long drive around the east perimeter of the course, known
as Manor Drive.

Within four years, Kevin Harris's bold experiment had
turned into a small goldmine. 'And just as well!' he'd told
Deborah with a sigh after his wife had returned from a shopping trip to Paris with enough parcels – and bills – to come
near to bankrupting him.

Such was the background to Deborah's thoughts and inten-
tions as she made her way hurriedly into the hotel foyer and
told the porter to telephone Mr Harris and ask him to meet
her in his office as a matter of great urgency. Pepe, the Spanish
concierge, raised his eyebrows as he looked at Miss Cahill's

bedraggled appearance. The woman he was accustomed to seeing was always immaculate, her hair scraped back in a bun, the tweed skirt perfectly pleated, her blouses Persil white, her cardigans shapeless but neatly buttoned. He had only once before seen her in comparative disarray, when she had returned from her after-breakfast walk having lost her precious dog. It turned out that the animal had rushed off after a passing bitch on heat which its owner had been walking on the 10th fairway and followed it home. Fortunately, the owner had seen the hotel telephone number on Rusty's collar, and calm had been restored when dog and owner were reunited. For the first time in very many years, Miss Cahill had not been at her desk at nine o'clock, and poor Mr Harris had been hard put to keep his temper, which he was only able to do because, he had informed Pepe, the wretched dog was the only creature the poor woman had to love.

Having tidied her hair and powdered her nose in the downstairs ladies' cloakroom, Deborah reached her office just as her boss arrived. He looked red faced and irritable as he demanded to know what possible reason she might have for insisting upon his presence at what was now nearly half past midnight.

'Couldn't you have called me on the phone?' he asked petulantly.

'Believe me, Mr Harris, you will understand when I tell you the reason I considered it preferable for you to be here rather than for me to telephone you in your room, where perhaps Mrs Harris might overhear what I have to tell you,' was Deborah's caustic reply.

Her voice was calm but Kevin knew her well enough to be aware it held a slight tremor. He ran a hand through his sparse grey hair and tried not to wonder whether Dolores would have let him make love to her if he'd not been called away just when he was about to get into bed with her. Probably not but . . .

'Mr Harris, there is a dead man at the bottom of the garden in the shrubbery between the hotel garden and the boundary wall. It's the Scot, Mr Gordon Rivers – the man you always mistake for an American because of his accent. I thought you should know before someone else finds him.'

Kevin's florid face paled.

'Good God, Debbie! Are you sure he's dead? You'd better phone the police. What on earth was the man doing out there?'

'I haven't the faintest idea, Mr Harris. However, on my way back to the hotel I started to wonder if you'd really want the police here at this time of night. I mean, sirens and lights and . . . well . . . there are eleven other guests in the hotel at the moment . . .'

Kevin stared at his assistant wide-eyed and with a not unusual admiration. Trust old Debs to keep her head and prevent him making a hash of things – something he'd have done heaven knows how many times before if she hadn't been there to extricate him! There was that occasion when the journalist female whose name he'd forgotten had come in drunk one night and propositioned the French chef who was as gay as they come and who had gone rushing into the bar asking the late-night drinkers to protect him. Fortunately, none of them spoke French and it had fallen to Deb, bless her, who was fluent in four languages, French being one of them, to calm the man down and get the randy journalist off to her room. Still, that was history. Now they had a really sticky problem on their hands. He looked at Deborah with his usual little-boy-lost expression, which never failed to work.

'What do you suggest we do?' he asked.

'I've been thinking. If between us we could go and fetch Mr Rivers, we could put him in the back of the hotel estate car. Then in an hour or so's time, when everyone in the hotel is asleep and we can be certain all the partygoers at the golf club will have gone home, we can drive him to Ferrybridge Hospital – pretend we'd found him on Manor Drive on one of the verges. That way, none of the guests would ever know anything unpleasant had happened at our hotel.'

Kevin let out his breath as he went to the cupboard below his bookshelf and took out a bottle of whisky he kept there for 'emergencies'. He was aware that his PA did not like spirits so poured out a generous tot for himself and drank it neat.

'Why don't we just leave him where he is – pretend you never saw him?'

'Think of the publicity, Mr Harris, if someone else found him!' Deborah replied quickly. *'Body found in Cheyne Manor Hotel gardens. Police are questioning guests and staff . . .'*

'Yes, yes, you're right of course,' Kevin broke in. 'But suppose some of the guests turned up just when we were fetching the . . . er . . . the body.' He paused to put his head in his hands and wondered whether he should have a second whisky to steady his nerves.

'The golf club party ended at midnight, Mr Harris. The hotel guests should be back by now but I'll check the key board just to see if all their keys have been picked up. Why don't you sit down for a minute and have another drink? I won't be long.'

'Bless you, my dear!' Kevin said with genuine appreciation, relieved to let his ever capable PA make the necessary decisions. When she did so, they were very rarely wrong, whereas when he thought something was for the best, invariably it wasn't; as so often his wife, Dolores, told him, her beautiful lush red lips curled in a disparaging downward curve of scorn. But even she could not deny that he had always made the right business decisions; that his financial acumen had been all but faultless. How else would he ever have made the kind of money to buy this place; build a superb golf course; have a timeshare in Marbella, which was where he had met Dolores Maria Carmen Ismenita, who he had married for her unquestionable sex appeal – and who had married him for his money.

There had been another reason she had agreed to marry him. It was because he owned a genuine English manor house and estate. Unaware that he had managed to purchase it at a knockdown price, she had assumed he came from the same aristocratic background as the previous owner, Sir Julian Matheson.

Buying the Cheyne Manor estate had been a gold star gamble, Kevin thought, and one which had won him the beautiful Dolores as a bonus prize. He'd thought he could live with the realization that his wife did not love him; but although Dolores' Catholic upbringing did not allow for a divorce, they had only been married a year before he discovered she had been unfaithful to him. It was to be the first of very many acts of adultery, but between the arrival and departure of the lovers who were able to satisfy her insatiable sexual appetite, she allowed him back into the marital bed. His adoration and lust for his wife came before his pride and the unspoken arrangement had become the status quo and was unlikely now ever to change.

Whilst Kevin had been mulling over the state of his marriage, Deborah had ascertained that all the guests had retired for the night. Most of them were golfers who would be up early and out on the course soon after breakfast. As for the pretty identical twin daughters of Julian Matheson, she had heard them moving about in the attic suite above her bedroom.

She looked at her wrist-watch. It was now almost a quarter to one.

'I suggest we wait another hour before we move him, Mr Harris,' Deborah said as she returned to his office. 'Just to be on the safe side.'

Kevin had had second thoughts whilst his PA had been absent.

'Why can't we just tip the body over the wall on to the golf course?' he suggested. 'The police would think one of the golfers killed him.'

There were now two pink patches on Deborah's cheeks and her heart was beating unnaturally fast as she realized excitedly how hugely important this moment was in her life. She was planning a course of action which would save her poor adored boss from all the stress and tension that would inevitably follow a murder investigation on the very doorstep of his beloved hotel. Her mind worked furiously.

'Because Mr Rivers has a very large lump on the back of

his head, which, if we leave him on the roadside, could easily have been caused by a car hitting him. The police will think it a case of hit-and-run rather than murder. Besides, if we did as you suggested they'd search the surrounding area and find the broken shrubs where the man's now lying. The publicity would be far greater for a murder than for a car accident.'

Kevin stood up and patted Deborah's shoulder.

'You're right, as always,' he said gratefully as he grasped the force of her argument. 'I agree. We should fetch him in an hour's time.'

Conscious of his proximity, Deborah caught her breath. How she loved him! She would do far more than this for him if it were needed.

'I don't suppose you'll be able to sleep, my dear, but try and get a bit of rest,' he told her. 'I must go and make sure Dolores doesn't wake, find me gone and get up to go looking for me whilst we're out of the hotel.'

His voice trailed off and Deborah looked quickly at the floor as they realized simultaneously that no way was Kevin's wife going to leave her comfortable bed in the early hours of the morning to go looking for her husband. As far as Dolores was concerned, he could drown in the lake by the eighteenth tee for all she would care – in fact, she might well be delighted to become a widow – a very rich widow . . .

Deborah's light touch on his arm brought Kevin's thoughts back to the present. He felt suprisingly comforted by her obvious devotion to him – a *friendly* devotion, he reminded himself, unwilling to believe Dolores' jeering comments that his prim little secretary was in love with him. Granted she had never married. Granted that there had been a suitor once, not long after he'd first employed her – a salesman from Croydon who'd wanted to marry her. But she'd turned him down, telling Kevin that her would-be husband had wanted her to go to Wales to live and that she would have had to give up her job, which she was unwilling to do. Kevin hadn't told Dolores this, knowing that she'd simply say this was yet another pointer to the fact that the poor girl was in love with him.

'I'll doze down here in the lounge,' he told her now. 'Don't want to disturb my wife. You'd better try and get some rest, Deborah.'

'I'll go and lie down,' she told him, knowing that it was extremely doubtful that she could relax, let alone doze as Kevin intended. They were, after all, about to act quite illegally. They should have notified the police immediately she'd found the body; and most definitely they should not move it. As she lay on her bed, wide eyed, she wondered for the first time if poor Mr Rivers really had been attacked, and, if so, who could possibly have wanted to kill him? As far as she was aware, he had led an uneventful life in Scotland as an engineer in a firm making generators. Apparently he'd decided to take early retirement and come to live in the south of England, where it was so much warmer. His Scottish relatives were all dead, he'd confided one evening when there was no one else in the bar and she had stopped to talk to him thinking he looked somewhat lonely. His one passion in life was golf, and he'd thought the south of England climate would give him more opportunities to play. Quite often, the pro found him a partner, but if one was not forthcoming he still enjoyed practising and had got his handicap down to single figures.

There was nothing really dislikeable about the fifty-year-old man yet Deborah had never really taken to him in the four months he had been living at Cheyne Manor Hotel. But he had always been perfectly polite, never got drunk or made lecherous inuendos as some of the younger golfers did. An inveterate snob, Deborah had little time for the hard-drinking, loud-mouthed, noisy groups who occasionally chose to take advantage of a 'special offer', cheap-priced weekend which included free green fees. She'd once told Kevin that if the decision was left to her she wouldn't have them in the place despite the revenue they brought in at a time of year when the hotel would be only half full. Despite the lack of income at that time, she knew Dolores had wanted him to buy her a new TVR sports car, of all wild extravagances. Nevertheless, Kevin had given her the car – a scorching red colour – for her birthday and Dolores swanned around in it attracting the men's envious glances as they admired not only the car but the driver.

The alarm by Deborah's bed startled her with its interruption to her reverie. Quickly tidying her grey hair, she pulled on a fleece-lined raincoat and slipped her feet into lace-up shoes. After telling the disappointed Rusty that he could not go with her, she returned him to his basket, shut the door and hurried downstairs. Kevin was stretched out on one of the leather sofas and was snoring softly. She stood for an instant staring down at him, wishing beyond anything that she could wake him with a kiss. The moment of weakness passed and she touched his shoulder.

'I've unlocked the garage door,' she told him as he sat up, 'so we can carry him straight in.'

'Clever girl – you've thought of everything!' Kevin said as he got wearily to his feet.

The rain had turned to a steady drizzle as together they crept along the gravelled path leading to the shrubbery. Kevin held a small pencil torch with which he tried ineffectually to guide them. Deborah, despite her waterproof coat, was shivering as she borrowed the torch to try to locate the body. Had it vanished? she asked herself fearfully.

But it was still there, the man's hair clinging to his scalp where a huge lump on the back of his head was clearly visible. Between gasps for air, they managed to extricate him from the undergrowth, and, with Kevin lifting his shoulders and Deborah his feet, they struggled back through the darkness, neither having a free hand now to hold the torch.

By the time they had manhandled Rivers' body into the back of the hotel's Volvo estate, Kevin's nerve had gone completely and even Deborah was trembling, unable to look at the slack jaw and staring eyes of the man she had been carrying.

Unlike a lot of other small hospitals, Ferrybridge still had an A & E department. At this pre-dawn hour, it was almost deserted. The duty doctor was woken and took only a moment to pronounce Mr Rivers well and truly dead, having almost certainly died from a severe blow to his head, which, according to the X-rays, had fractured his skull. A post-mortem would doubtless confirm this, the doctor said cheerfully. Meanwhile the police had been informed by the staff nurse on duty and a police constable was waiting to talk to them in the visitors' room.

'It really would have been a lot better for you to have left the poor chap where you found him,' the policeman said as Kevin tried to explain that Miss Cahill had thought it would be most uncharitable to leave the man lying in the rain on the side of the road.

'It was quite a shock for her,' he elaborated.

At this point Deborah took over, fearing that Kevin might not remember the story they had agreed on.

'I was walking my little dog, Rusty,' she explained. 'I always take him out last thing before I go to bed – that is around midnight. As it had been raining earlier this evening and the grass was wet I didn't stay out very long. Later Rusty woke me up needing to go out again, so, rather than go out in the wet garden, I took him down the road, Manor Drive, leading to the golf club. That's when Rusty found him.'

The middle-aged policeman regarded Deborah's white, exhausted face and said apologetically: 'It must have been quite a shock for you, Miss . . . er . . . Cahill. What did you do next?'

'I hurried back to the hotel and fortunately Mr Harris, the owner, was still up – there was a party at the golf club last night so the guests were quite late coming back – the guests who are staying at the hotel, that is. Mr Rivers would have been one of them.' She paused briefly before adding, 'Mr Harris and I decided we couldn't leave Mr Rivers lying there in case another car hit him so Mr Harris went back to the hotel to fetch the hotel car and we put him in and drove the poor man here.'

As the policeman made notes in his book, Kevin looked at Deborah admiringly. She had sounded utterly convincing in her precise, clipped voice. Like the policeman, he would not have doubted her.

'Can you describe exactly where you found the body?' the policeman asked.

For a moment, neither Kevin nor Deborah spoke. Deborah found her voice first.

'It was much nearer the clubhouse than the hotel,' she said, 'but I'm afraid I can't be exact. There are chestnut trees all the way on either side of the road. It used to be a driveway, you see, from the manor house to the club, which was the dower house. I suppose I had been out about five or ten minutes but I can't be certain how far I'd got as Rusty likes to stop and sniff the trees.'

'Did you notice many cars on the road, miss, seeing as how there was this party at the club?' the constable asked, wishing that all witnesses were as precise as this woman.

'Well, not at that time of night,' Deborah replied. 'But the festivities ended at midnight so there would have been a lot of cars earlier.'

The policeman finished his notes and, thanking his two witnesses, informed them that he would be handing over to a detective inspector in the morning.

'No point getting him out of bed at this hour!' he said jocularly as they all left the room and started to walk down the corridor towards the main door. 'I expect he'll be up to see you at the hotel first thing. With a bit of luck, the post-mortem will be done tomorrow and that should tell us whether a car or an assailant hit the gentleman.'

'An assailant?' Kevin repeated uneasily. 'You mean someone might . . . might have killed him? Mr Rivers? We thought it was a typical hit-and-run case.'

The policeman shrugged.

'You never know, do you, sir? The doctor said the X-rays showed a severe blow to the back of the skull and bruising on the upper body. He said they could possibly be the result of the wing mirror of a large vehicle hitting him as it came from behind him, but, equally, he could have been struck by a weapon such as a piece of wood. However, Detective Inspector Govern will look into it.'

'I do hope he will be discreet!' Deborah said anxiously. 'Our guests won't like a murder inquiry on the doorstep.'

The policeman smiled reassuringly.

'You may rely on Inspector Govern's tactfulness,' he said. 'He's a really good bloke and so is his sergeant, DS Beck. You'll meet them tomorrow. They will probably want to go through the gentleman's effects. I understand he was a resident at your hotel.'

As they walked out of the hospital into the car park and Kevin opened the door for Deborah, he could see the police car as it drove away, the blue light on the roof no longer flashing. He started the engine and was halfway back to the hotel before either of them spoke. Then he said with a faint tremor in his voice, 'I checked the wing mirror just now. There's no way it could have hit someone on the back of the head. It's not much more than a metre high, and it's the only thing that sticks out!'

For a moment, Deborah was too shocked to think of a reply. She knew very little about cars, but even so, she could see that a wing mirror was never going to strike someone on the head albeit Mr Rivers was little more than five foot eight inches tall.

'Maybe a lorry? A van?' she volunteered.

Kevin let out his breath, a faint hope reviving at Deborah's suggestion. But his innate pessimism quickly diminished his hopes.

'Suppose the pathologist says it couldn't have been a vehicle that killed Rivers? Deb, has it sunk in? They'll think that you saying you'd found him in the road was a lie. They'll know it wasn't a hit-and-run and that, after all, it must have been murder. We'll have moved him for nothing.'

The same thought had been going through Deborah's mind but she saw no point in allowing Kevin to panic.

'Even if they do suspect a murder, they aren't going to find out we moved him, Mr Harris,' she said. 'No one saw us do it and there is no other way they can possibly connect us to Mr Rivers' death. Even if he was killed, it certainly wasn't by us.'

21

Three

Neither of the girls slept well. Both woke several times during the night and, once, were convinced they had heard movements. Neither voiced their nocturnal fears that somehow it was the ghost of Gordon Rivers, if not the man himself, come to haunt them.

As they got out of bed and went to stand at the twin basins in their bathroom, Rose said suddenly: 'It's no good, Pops, we've just got to report what happened and take the consequences. Don't you see, the boys knew we left early and took the short cut. It has to be pretty obvious you or I had something to do with . . . with *his* death.' She couldn't bring herself to speak Gordon Rivers' name aloud. 'After we've had breakfast, I'll ring the police station – ask to speak to someone senior. They must have an inspector there who'll be understanding.'

Poppy regarded her twin anxiously.

'I know how you're feeling, Rose, and of course I agree, but don't you think we ought to phone Papa first?'

Rose put down her hairbrush and sat down on the vanity stool. Her legs were trembling and she felt sick. Their father was such a pillar of rectitude, how could they possibly expect him to understand? Of course he would have wanted Gordon Rivers punished, imprisoned; but not killed; and certainly not by one of his daughters.

'Maybe it won't be necessary and the police won't charge me, arrest me!' she said, suspecting as did Poppy that the consequences were inevitable.

Poppy put an arm round her shoulders.

'Come on, Rose, let's have breakfast. We'll be feeling stronger if we eat something.' She knew Rose had no more appetite than she did but it was common knowledge that people's brains worked better if they started the day with a substantial meal – and they were going to need their wits if they were to have a hope of extricating themselves from this nightmare. One thing was certain, she would not allow Rose to say it was she who had hit Rivers over the head and killed him. It was, after all, *her* golf club, and she'd say *she*, Poppy, had done it; that she'd picked up the club when Rose was arriving on the scene and hit Rivers when he had turned to see who it was.

'Don't you see, Rose, they won't be able to prove which one of us hit him. Everyone knows you can't convict a person if there's a doubt.' As they went down the wide staircase and entered the dining room they heard an unusual buzz of conversation. One of the two old ladies who wintered in Spain but spent the spring and summer at the hotel caught hold of Poppy's arm.

'Have you heard the news, dear? It's given Ida and me quite a shock. You know that man who usually sits over there by the window, Mr Rivers his name is. Or should I say "was"? Well, he's been killed.'

Poppy felt Rose's hand tighten on her arm as a shaft of fear went through her. The shock must have shown on both their faces for the other old lady tut-tutted as she chided her friend Hilda.

'You've frightened them, you silly besom!' she said. She turned back to the twins. 'Don't worry, dears, it wasn't a proper murder. Pepe spoke to one of the policemen who was in Manor Drive. They've cordoned off the side where they think the body was found. The policeman told our waiter it was almost certainly a hit-and-run.'

'Some drunken lout driving too fast, I don't doubt,' Hilda said primly. 'Pepe told us that so much beer was drunk at that party last night, the bar steward had to come to the hotel for further supplies, but he hadn't seen a body. But I mustn't keep you two dear girls from your breakfast.' She looked roguishly at the twins. 'Have a nice day – as the shop girls say!' she added.

Speechless, the twins made their way to their usual table at the far end of the room. Rose spoke first.

'Ida said he'd been found in Manor Drive. Oh, Poppy,' she added in a whisper, 'suppose he wasn't dead and after we'd gone he got up and staggered across the course to the road for help.'

Poppy clasped her hands together beneath the table in an attempt to stop them trembling.

'Don't be silly, Rose! He could never have walked that far – and, anyway, if he'd only been knocked unconscious he'd still never have been able to negotiate the bridge on to the seventeenth, then over the sixteenth green and right across the fifteenth to get to Manor Drive.'

'And it would have been miles quicker for him to go straight into the hotel and ask for help,' Rose concluded. 'No, he was dead, Pops, I'm absolutely *sure* of it.'

They stopped talking whilst the Spanish waiter, a relation of Pepe's, came to take their order. Both girls declined a cooked breakfast, surprising the waiter, who was used to bringing them eggs, bacon, sausages, fried bread and baked beans. Not that either one showed signs of becoming over-weight. Both were slim enough for him to consider they needed feeding up. In his country, he said to Pepe, the women looked like women, not like young lads.

He was called away to another hotel guest who had come down for breakfast, and Deborah Cahill came over to the twins' table. As far as they could see, she seemed to be doing the rounds.

'I expect you've both heard the sad news about poor Mr Rivers,' she said in quiet, measured tones. 'As far as we know it does look as if he was hit by a van or a truck on his way back to the hotel last night. We know it wasn't a car because most wing mirrors on modern cars today fly back on impact, and besides, they would be too low to catch the back of someone's head. On heavy goods vehicles, nearly all are fixed. However, we shall know more after the post-mortem. Meanwhile, a Detective Inspector Govern will be coming to the hotel presently to ask some routine questions. Until then, he has requested that none of the guests leaves the premises. I'm sorry if you two girls have booked a game of golf and have to cancel it.'

Somehow, Rose managed to pull herself together. She attempted a smile.

'It's okay, thanks, Miss Cahill. We'd be cancelling anyway because Poppy sprained her ankle.'

Deborah Cahill quite liked the twins, who were always polite, and having been reassured that Poppy did not need to see the doctor to look at her ankle she moved on to the next guests, a party of men who had arrived as a society from the Midlands and were due to tee off at ten o'clock. They were inclined to argue with Deborah until she told them that, in any event, the golf course had been closed for play by the police whilst everyone was questioned.

Muttering that they would be demanding their money back, the party of men got up and went through to the old billiard room, now used for snooker.

At precisely ten o'clock, Inspector Govern arrived with his detective sergeant, a nice-looking, youngish man also in plain clothes. By now, Deborah had shepherded all the hotel guests and staff into the lounge, where the inspector addressed them.

'Instead of asking you all to come down to the police station in Ferrybridge, I will take a statement from each of you here. This is a mere formality so that we can eliminate you all from the enquiry into Mr Rivers' death. At this stage, we think it is possible that the gentleman was hit by a truck coming up the road, Manor Drive, from the direction of the golf club.'

He glanced around the groups, who were listening to him intently.

'I do emphasize that this is an informal routine questioning. As you probably know, Mr Rivers died as a result of a blow to his head and no one has reported an accident, so we need to check any vehicles which might have been on the road late last night. Will those of you with vehicles be so good as to give your names to DS Beck and answer a few simple questions – its make, if you drove to and from the clubhouse last night, where I understand there was a party, and at what time – that sort of thing. We will try not to delay you too long!'

'Any delay is too long!' one of the Midlanders said with a smirk in an undertone and his friends grinned.

'One of those clever so-and-sos!' David Beck muttered. 'Let's get him out of the way first!'

The questioning began, mainly who left the clubhouse at what time of the evening and whether anyone was with them or saw them leave. The twins, along with one or two other hotel guests, remained silent, having agreed beforehand that Rose should postpone her confession for the time being. If no one was unjustly accused of being the hit-and-run driver, there might be no need to say anything at all, they had decided. These hopes were dashed, however, when after all the car owners had given their statements, Inspector Govern said: 'As you know, at the present time it would appear that Mr Rivers was hit by a wing mirror, as he sustained injuries to the back of his head. The time was probably somewhere between eleven and midnight. There will be a post-mortem this afternoon and if – as could happen – the pathologist tells us it is not certain that the injuries to Mr Rivers came from a vehicle but that they may have been caused by some other instrument, then the situation will become considerably more serious. At the moment, as I said, we think it was an accident. If, however, any one of you knows of a reason why someone might have wanted Mr Rivers dead, will they please contact me or DS Beck as soon as possible. Anything said to me or to my sergeant will be treated entirely confidentially. If necessary, a simple phone call will suffice. Sergeant Beck will give you the direct phone number to my desk at the station.' He glanced at the sea of anxious faces and added, 'Those I have spoken to are free to leave now. Would those

I still have not questioned please remain for a little longer while we talk to Mr Harris and his assistant? Thank you for your patience and cooperation.'

He and his sergeant left the room and followed Deborah Cahill into Kevin's office. Kevin got to his feet and coughed nervously.

'Do sit down, Inspector!' he said, pointing to the chair usually occupied by Deborah. 'I'm quite willing to be questioned, of course, but I don't think I can tell you anything more than we said at the hospital last night. As I said, Miss Cahill deals directly with the guests, and has far more contact with them than I do. I . . . well, I try and keep out of the way.' He gave a sickly smile and nodded to Sergeant Beck.

Before the inspector could begin questioning her or her boss, Deborah said quickly: 'Mr Rivers was Scottish, you know. He came to spend a summer holiday here with us two years ago and liked it so much he decided to come and live here when he retired, which he did last Christmas. He was a very neat man, meticulous about his possessions, and I don't think he can have had any monetary worries because he always paid his bills extremely promptly.'

Govern listened to Deborah's quiet, efficient summary and decided he could do with a secretary like her. As David had said earlier, she might not have good legs, a pretty face or a figure to die for, to use his sergeant's description, but he had little doubt that it was she who ran the hotel, not the nervous little hotel owner-manager.

'At the hospital you said that as far as you knew Mr Rivers had no wife or relatives,' Govern said, 'so we'll have to go through his effects and see if we can find a lead of some sort to his next of kin. You did lock the room as I asked, Miss Cahill?'

Of course she had! David thought. She wasn't the sort to forget anything, including elevenses.

'I took the liberty of ordering coffee for everyone,' she was saying as one of the waitresses came into the office with a tray of cups and biscuits.

27

'Very thoughtful, thank you!' Govern said, noting the visible relaxation of Kevin Harris's body. Surely the insignificant little man can't have anything to hide, he thought, yet he kept glancing at the door in the oddest fashion.

The explanation was not long in coming. A tall, buxom, colourful woman swept into the office without knocking. Her raven-black hair was swept high on the back of her head; her equally black eyes were heavily ringed with mascara and her full-lipped mouth was a vivid red. She might have been an opera diva the way she carried herself so imperiously, Govern decided.

Staring straight at him, she spoke in heavily accented English. 'Why was I not informed you police people was here?' she demanded, and, turning to her husband, said accusingly, 'You think I don'ta want to know which is happening when that poor man is died? You think I am the idiot and will have the hys-tericks?' As she paused to draw breath, Sergeant Beck thought with an inward grimace, she might not have 'the hystericks' but I will if she goes on much longer. He could see his boss was about to speak, but the woman, who he now gathered must be Harris's wife, was not yet prepared to give up the stage.

''Ave you told this policeman that I was 'aving the very long talk in the bar with Señor Rivers before the poor man went off to the fiesta? Very nice señor. He was not happy when I told him you had said we could not go to the golf party. When I told him I am the best tango performer in Madrid, he had wished very much to dance with me.' She looked from the inspector to Sergeant Beck and smiled provocatively at the good-looking younger man. 'Here now in England the tango dance is popular, is it not so, and—'

She broke off as Kevin Harris interrupted her.

'May I introduce my wife?' he said apologetically, and to his wife he said, 'Dolores, we are in conference at the moment, my dear. Perhaps these two gentlemen would like to hear about the tango at some future date?'

Dolores' smile faded and her expression became sulky.

'You English people think all the times only of work, work, work . . .' she complained. 'In my country we sing and dance and enjoy our persons. Very well, I will leave you. Anyways, I wish to take the car in to Ferrybridge, Kevin, to do some shopping.'

'I'm afraid that won't be possible this morning!' Govern said. 'CSI will be coming up to inspect all the vehicles here and at the golf club.' He looked at Kevin and added apologetically: 'Of course, we know your hotel car was on the road, Mr Harris, as you fetched the body. But we'll need to check the tyres for elimination purposes.'

Dolores threw up her hands, her eyes flashing. Kevin had told her first thing this morning that Deborah had gone to look for Rusty and found the body in the road, and that together they had gone to the hospital. After midnight, too! Had Deborah Cahill been anyone else but a late-middle-aged, plain, skinny stick of a woman she might have thought her husband was up to no good. He was always wanting to make love but his performances were so inadequate for her pleasure that more often than not she refused him. Anxious for sex though her husband might be, she could not imagine he would have been taking Deborah for an illicit drive! But for Deborah to go looking for a dog . . . well, all the English were quite mad so Kevin's story was possible. As for herself . . . if that handsome young sergeant were available . . .

'For the second time, Dolores, would you be so good as to leave us to our discussions?' Kevin's voice, sharpened by his taut nerves, regained her attention, which had been focused on Sergeant Beck. She was always flirting with young men – guests in the hotel, people in shops, in car parks . . . anywhere where someone took her fancy. Big breasted, she wore low-cut dresses, her whole demeanour flamboyant, sexually provocative. It was, Kevin realized, why he himself had first been attracted to her. Even now, all these years later and despite her ill-concealed deprecation of him, he still wanted her.

Having taken note of the relationship between the hotel

manager and his exotic wife, Inspector Govern now returned
to the other hotel residents, leaving his sergeant in Miss Cahill's
care to make a careful search of Gordon Rivers' room. He
spoke briefly to the two elderly women, Ida Smithers and her
companion, Hilda Nutting, hoping they might be more inform-
ative about the dead man if he approached them informally.
But neither could add to the little they had told him – simply
that Mr Rivers had once referred to an aunt who lived in
Edinburgh and had since died, leaving him a small legacy.
This had enabled him to retire from his job, which they seemed
to recall was connected in some way with an engineering firm
in the north of Scotland. Their memories were far too vague
to be of any use to Govern, who then went across the room
to talk to the twins.

Like everyone else who had come into contact with them
since their babyhood, he was intrigued by their exact image
of one another. This morning, however, one of the girls had
her ankle bandaged and was resting it on a stool.

'I'm Poppy Matheson,' she told him, seeing his confusion.
'This is Rose!'

Govern smiled.

'I believe you told my sergeant, DS Beck, that you were
the one who left the party early?'

Poppy nodded.

'But Rose left too, as soon as she knew I'd gone, and she
caught up with me before I got to the hotel.'

'If I remember correctly, you both thought the time was
around eleven p.m.? I suppose you didn't hear anything untoward – a vehicle braking or accelerating?'

The girls shook their heads.

'The short cut is quite a long way from Manor Drive,' Rose
said. 'I don't suppose we would have heard anything from
where we were.'

Govern had been out earlier that morning with David Beck,
who had shown him round the clubhouse, and he'd had a brief
glimpse of the golf course itself. It was still possible to see
that the land could once all have been part of Cheyne Manor

estate – the old trees, the three lakes and the streams running between them. David had said there might still be carp or trout in them. It must have been a wrench for the girls when their father sold out to Harris, as the redoubtable Miss Cahill had informed him. They seemed unusually quiet, reserved for twenty-year-old students; but then the unfortunate Mr Rivers' death had probably unnerved them. Rivers had, after all, been a resident at the hotel like themselves and doubtless they'd known him quite well.

When he now suggested this, both girls nodded, but each was sharing the same thought – that they'd never liked him. Whenever they'd been in the same room with him, he always stared at them. Rose had once accused him of doing so, telling him bluntly that they'd been brought up not to stare because it was rude. He'd laughed off the reproof, blaming their shared identity for his need to keep looking. Once Poppy had been paired with him in a mixed foursome tournament and she'd deliberately played so badly that they were beaten five and four and she was able to get back to the clubhouse much earlier than expected.

They made no mention of this to Govern, who remained at the hotel long enough to chat to the other residents before Sergeant Beck reappeared. Although he'd found no names of anyone who might be Rivers' next-of-kin, he had found some bank statements relating to an account in a bank in Edinburgh from which they could get further details.

Whilst both detectives made their way to the clubhouse for further investigations, the hotel was permitted to open its doors, and as soon as Pepe had done so, John and Fred came hurrying in. They went immediately to the lounge where Pepe had told them they would find the girls. Fred bent and kissed Poppy's cheek. He sat down in a chair beside her.

'I don't know how to tell you how awful I've been feeling ever since the policeman at the top of the road stopped us and told us what was going on. I should never have let you go home on your own, Poppy. I'd never have forgiven myself if anything had happened to you.'

31

For a moment, neither twin spoke, then Poppy managed to give him a weak smile.

'Nothing did happen to me, did it? The inspector thinks Mr Rivers was almost certainly hit by a truck. Miss Cahill found him on the road to the clubhouse and she and Mr Harris took him to hospital.'

'Maybe the driver didn't know they'd hit him,' John said charitably.

'Let's not talk about it,' Rose suggested. 'Let's decide what we're going to do today. The golf course is closed and Poppy can't play tennis.'

John suggested they take the train up to London and go to a show.

'My treat!' he said, as always generous with the large allowance his wealthy father gave him. As John had once told the girls, his parent was too busy adding to his vast chain of sports shops dotted all over America to play the father role adequately, so salvaged his conscience by paying huge sums of money into his anglophile son's account.

Although John was an only child, his father had been perfectly agreeable to his son's wish to go to England to study for his Masters, or, indeed, to fulfil any other desire he might have. John had written to tell his parents about the English girl, Rose, whom he was crazy about and wanted to take home to introduce to them. Since they'd met last October, Rose had seemed more than happy to let their relationship deepen into something more serious and, with another year to go before he completed his studies, he was content with the status quo. Now Rose immediately jumped at the suggestion of a show. Provided Poppy's ankle was not worrying her, she thought, to get away from the hotel would at least help to take their minds off last night's horrific events. Upstairs in their room, where they went to change their clothes, they had a few moments alone to talk about their situation.

'Somehow, God alone knows how, someone moved Gordon Rivers' body from the bushes where we hid him,' Poppy said bleakly as she put on her new Diesel jeans and T-shirt.

'Whoever found him must have taken him to Manor Drive and dumped him, but why?'

'What's even more astonishing,' Rose said, 'was Miss Cahill finding him on the road and she and Mr Harris taking him to hospital.'

'Maybe he was still alive!' Poppy whispered once more, but Rose shook her head.

'He was dead, Pops,' she said. 'I know it's unbelievable that he got to the road – but it actually happened. I just can't see how.'

Poppy was equally nonplussed, but she had been so consumed with fear for Rose having to face a charge of murder, she now welcomed these new events with immense relief. Rose must be mistaken and Gordon Rivers had been alive when they'd tipped him over the wall, she thought. He'd regained consciousness and wandered across the golf course on to the road. There, some unknown person had driven into him and killed him. It was the only explanation, so there was no need now to confess to their father; no need to confess to the police. All they had to do was to keep silent – and all would be well.

'As you know, David, I had my doubts about this case being a hit-and-run,' Inspector Govern told his sergeant as they left Cheyne Manor Hotel and drove down to the golf club. 'But after what you've just told me, perhaps that *was* the cause of Rivers' death.'

Sergeant Beck had taken it upon himself to arrange for a DC in the CID office to check with a local second-hand car dealer what kind of vehicle might have a wing mirror positioned high enough to hit the back of a pedestrian's head. A call had now come through on his mobile saying that a VW truck fitted the bill provided the pedestrian was no taller than five foot eight. There could be other vehicles whose mirrors were similarly positioned and checks were being carried out.

'Although what a VW truck was doing at midnight on

the road to the clubhouse is questionable,' Govern added thoughtfully.

'Not everyone can afford a BMW like yours, sir!' David said grinning. 'Could be someone at the party asked a friend with a truck to pick them up.'

'Not very likely,' Govern replied. 'However, the driver may not have known about the dance. The road to the clubhouse must be pretty deserted at night . . .'

'And it would be the perfect place for a spot of nookey!'

Govern swung the car into the visitors' car park.

'Called it "necking" in my day,' he said. 'You could be right. We'll have to see.'

He and David Beck had been working together as a team for the past three years and, although they were in many ways close friends, both men observed the difference in their ranks and Beck never overstepped the mark.

'If we get this case wrapped up before the weekend, maybe I can get a game here,' Beck said, looking with interest at the neatly cut fairway of the first hole to the left of the car park.

Inspector Govern smiled.

'Sometimes, David, the simplest-looking cases turn out to be the most difficult to untangle. Remember the Millers Lane murders? Took us weeks to sort them out. So don't count your golf balls before you're teed up, right?'

'Didn't know you knew the terminology, sir!' David said, laughing, as they pulled up outside the clubhouse. Not that his boss had quoted the proverb correctly – but he knew what he meant.

Many of the people at the club had been at the dance the previous night. By the time they had finished questioning them it was nearly four o'clock. Govern was enjoying a cup of tea when he received a phone call from the police station to say that the pathologist who'd performed the post-mortem had not ruled out the possibility that the unfortunate Mr Rivers had been hit on the back of the head by the wing mirror of a passing vehicle, and that such a blow could have killed him. The victim had been over the drink driving limit apparently, and, as Govern had suggested, he could have lurched sideways as the vehicle drove past him. Nevertheless the post-mortem examination had shown surprisingly little bruising to the rest of the body other than to the man's shoulders. The time of death was estimated to be between ten and midnight, and tallied with the statements of those who had been at the bar in the clubhouse stating that they had not seen Rivers after eleven. The bar steward and several other people reported that he'd been drinking quite heavily earlier in the evening.

As they left the now almost deserted clubhouse, Govern said: 'Apart from the heavy drinking, it seems Mr Rivers was a quiet, reserved man who kept himself to himself. Always paid his bill promptly, according to the redoubtable Miss Cahill.'

David nodded.

'Very much a loner, sir. I never heard a single person mention friends – or enemies come to that.'

Govern frowned.

'It fits the supposition that his death was an accident and there was no foul play. I just wish more people understood that if ever they come upon a dead person, or even an injured person, come to that, on no account should they move them. I don't think Harris realized it was an offence to move a dead body.'

'You'd think he and the old girl would have known it, though, wouldn't you, sir?' Beck said as they drove back to Ferrybridge. 'What's the betting one or other of them bashed him over the head and then dumped him on the side of the road to cover up the murder?'

Govern laughed.

'Trouble with you, David, is you read too many detective novels! Has it crossed your mind there has to be a motive for murder? A pretty good one, too. Next you'll be telling me Harris and his PA were having an affair and Rivers found out and threatened to tell his wife!'

It was David Beck's turn to grin.

'What, humping that Cahill spinster when he could be bedding the glorious Dolores?'

'That's quite enough, DS Beck!' the older man said sternly, but, despite himself, he too was smiling.'

Four

'So what happened to you, Rose? You and Jason should have won your match easily.'

Having been allotted early starts, both Poppy and Rose had completed their rounds in the annual mixed foursome handicap tournament and were now in the ladies' changing room. It had been hot on the course and, having removed their shoes and clothes, they had showered before changing into clean T-shirts and striped cotton trousers. Sonia Turner, the wife of the club captain, had preceded them and left the room.

'Now we're on our own, Poppy,' Rose said, 'I can tell you what happened. On the fifth I shanked my drive, scuffed my three wood, and *four* putted. The wretched Jason Armitage was clearly appalled. When he asked me to be his partner, I think he'd been hoping we'd manage a decent score. Pops, it's getting worse, not better. I simply can't play that hole. It gives me the creeps!'

Poppy pulled the T-shirt down over her waist and put a comforting arm round her twin's shoulders.

'I know. I feel it, too. I keep thinking Gordon Rivers is going to appear suddenly from those bushes. I suppose we're both lifting our heads to make sure he or his ghost isn't there!'

Rose hunched her shoulders and despite the warmth of the room she shivered.

'I actually thought I saw someone today beneath that big beech tree, but it was only a branch. Poppy, do you believe there are such things as ghosts? Do you think he could come back and haunt us?'

Poppy did her best to look convincing as she said firmly: 'No, I don't – and, anyway, you were only trying to save me when you used my club to hit him. You didn't *mean* to kill him, Rose, and what's more Rivers deserved to die. What about those other women? I'll never forget his horrible voice saying I wanted him . . . was asking him to . . .' Her voice had become unsteady and now failed altogether.

Rose said quickly: 'We really must try and forget it, Poppy. Maybe we should move right away from here. We could tell Papa we've changed our minds and want to go to a French university. It's what he wanted when we badgered him to let us go to Sussex. What do you think?'

Poppy drew a long sigh and stood up in order to regard herself in the mirror above the wash basin.

'In one way that's a good idea, but we'd lose touch with John and Fred . . .'

Rose nodded. She knew Poppy was as attracted to Fred as she was to John. The four of them had even talked vaguely about sharing a flat in Ferrybridge next year. Meanwhile, they had decided to wait and see if what had started as a mild flirtation would grow into something more. As far as the twins were concerned, they'd not yet had nor wanted a live-in relationship. Apart from needing a member of the opposite sex to satisfy their sexual urges, they were everything they needed to each other.

Two more players now came into the changing room and the conversation became general until, five minutes later, the twins left to go off to the bar for a drink with their playing partners and opponents. Neither, therefore, was aware that all the time they had believed they were alone there had been a third player, Betty Russell, in one of the toilets.

While the girls had been showering, Betty had answered the call of nature and was still in the cubicle when they had started conversing, their clear, girlish voices audible to her despite the fact that they were speaking quietly. She was doing no more than considering the hazards of the 5th green, which the twins appeared to dislike, when she was riveted by the remark that followed Rose's comments.

Betty had been on the point of leaving the cubicle when Poppy's voice reached her ears: '*You didn't mean to kill him, Rose.*' Shocked beyond movement, she had collapsed on to the seat of the toilet and put her hand over her mouth to still the gasps that were stuck in her throat. Could she possibly have misheard what the girl had said? she asked herself – *Kill him . . . Rivers . . .* Gordon Rivers? But that didn't make sense. He'd been a hit-and-run victim. His body had been found on the side of Manor Drive, nowhere near the fifth green.

Suddenly the middle-aged woman became frightened to move lest the twins realize she was in the room with them and must have heard their conversation. Obviously they had had no idea she was in the toilet and had supposed she'd left when Sonia Turner had departed. She could do nothing but remain where she was and hope that the girls would leave without noticing her closed door.

Two other women arrived, one entering the cubicle adjoining hers. When she could no longer hear the twins' voices and after waiting another few minutes she decided it would be safe to emerge. With a sigh of relief, she saw that the twins had left.

Her legs trembling, Betty decided not to stay for a drink or the subsequent prize-giving ceremony and to go straight home. If she stayed, her husband, Barry, would notice at once that something was wrong and could even draw attention to it without realizing the danger it might put her in. If the twins really had killed Gordon Rivers then once they suspected she had overheard them she could be their next victim. She would go home and wait for Barry before calling the police.

It was not surprising that when she first explained to her husband the reason why she had rushed home without first telling him, he laughed in her face and pooh-poohed the suggestion of an actual murder. His voice was scornful as he went across the room to pour himself a whisky, saying: 'How bloody ridiculous can you get, woman? I really do begin to wonder sometimes if you're quite all there. Or maybe you've started the menoclause – or whatever it is you women call it. Rose and Poppy Matheson bumping off poor old Rivers? You really must be loco!'

Usually, when he adopted that critical, hectoring tone she left the room, but now her anxiety overcame her distress. She had known for many years that her husband had never loved her; that he had married her for her money and that he took a sadistic pleasure in belittling her. She had once read in a woman's magazine that men with inferiority complexes were known to bully and belittle their wives in order to feel superior; that the more the wife tolerated this behaviour, the more frequently they indulged in it. Nevertheless, she still loved him, if not with the same passionate devotion of their early years.

In those days Betty had allowed him full access to her private account, which, at his request on their honeymoon, she had made a joint account. But his endless extravagances had slowly depleted the legacy her parents had left their only daughter, and on the advice of her bank manager she had had his name removed. When Barry discovered what she had done he had at first been furiously angry, then threatened to leave her, and finally been obliged to accept her suggestion that she would pay him an allowance. Despite the fact that she had by then been forced to realize that he was both a wastrel and, where she was concerned, a bully, she continued to love him and would have been devastated had he carried out his threat and left her.

Her voice was quiet and very controlled as she turned now and said: 'Barry, you have to believe what I am telling you, however unbelievable it is – and I understand why you think so. I could hardly believe my own ears. But the girls went on talking – very quietly, of course. They said they were frightened and spoke of going away to live in France.'

Barry sat down in the armchair he favoured and stared at his wife over the rim of his glass, considering for the hundredth time how plain she was with her long nose, short, frizzy grey hair and close-set eyes.

'You've got the wrong end of the stick, my girl. Of course

they knew you were in the bog and they were having you on. It was all a stupid joke, and like a fool you fell for it.'

Betty remained standing, for once indifferent to the disparaging tone of his remark.

'I would swear on the Holy Bible that those girls were in deadly earnest—' She broke off, uneasy with the adjective she'd inadvertently used, but she now repeated it: 'They were deadly serious, frightened!' she said. 'I would say one of them was not far from tears. Barry, it's inconceivable they would invent a story about killing someone. Besides, even if you were right and they had known someone was in the loo they wouldn't have known who it was. Don't you see, I was already in there when they came in.'

'So you're saying they just walked in and started whingeing about having killed a man? Pull the other one, Betty!'

Somehow, she kept calm.

'No, Barry, they undressed and were having a shower when I went into the loo. It was when they came out to put on their clothes that they started talking.'

'And you were in the bog all that time?'

'Yes, I was. I'd had a bit of a tummy upset – I think it must have been those mussels we had for supper last night. Anyway, I felt sick and I thought I should stay where I was just in case. I just stood there – that's why I wasn't making any noise. I was about to come out when I heard one of the twins say she didn't mean to kill Gordon. Believe me, Barry, it was no joke. She would have had to be an exceptionally good actress to make her voice tremble like that.'

Momentarily, Barry was beset by uncertainty, his ridicule tempered by the measured tone of his wife's voice. Stupid as Betty was, this particular story was too ridiculous for even her to have invented it. But the Matheson twins? How could they possibly have killed a grown man like Gordon Rivers? And why? And, anyway, he'd been hit by a car on Manor Drive. What was all the nonsense about being scared of ghosts on the fifth fairway?

'Shouldn't we call the police, Barry? I know at the inquest

41

they said it had been a hit-and-run accident, but maybe it wasn't. Maybe—'

'No!' Barry's voice was as hard as the expression on his face. 'Do you honestly think they'd believe you? You'd look a right idiot going to them with a story like that. Besides, what proof can you offer them? None – because you have none. It's your word against the girls'. I know who I'd believe – and it wouldn't be you. Women of your age do get funny ideas. My Aunt Hazel . . . well, no point bringing her into it, but they put her in a looney bin.'

For a moment, Betty remained silent. By now, if this had been one of his usual tirades, she would have long since left the room. He was a little surprised to see her still confronting him.

'Barry, if those girls *have* killed someone, they might well kill again, and if we don't warn the police it would be our fault.'

Her husband gave a short caustic laugh.

'And if we do tell the police what was said – and we haven't any way of substantiating it – and the two murderesses get to hear about it, they might come and bump us off! Although you wouldn't be such a loss to humanity, I certainly don't intend to kick the bucket just when I've reached retirement age. No thank you very much. And I'll thank you not to go yelling your head off in the club – or anywhere else, come to that. Just keep your mouth shut for once – if you can. We all know you're addicted to gossiping. It's common knowledge in the club.'

Betty caught her breath, her heart bruising at his criticism although she knew she should be used to it by now. Slowly she left the room and went upstairs, where she found her way through a mist of tears to her dressing table. There, as always, was the triptych photograph frame containing their wedding photographs. Sometimes she wondered why she still displayed them, so long was it since that day when she had still believed he loved her. Deep down, despite her sadness, she didn't want to discard them. Barry had done his best to destroy her self-confidence, and her best friend, Joan, now far away in Australia, had said: *'I can't think why you stay with him, Betty. You know he doesn't love you. Come to Australia with Jack and me . . .'*

But by then she had come to terms with Barry's lack of love for her, and in a way she still loved him. It was an addiction, like smoking, she once told herself. People knew smoking was bad for them and would have liked not to want a cigarette, but the desire was always there.

Maybe Joan was right when she had suggested she should go and see Paul McKenna and get him to hypnotize her. *'When you wake up, you will no longer want to live with your husband. You will no longer kid yourself that he does need you, does love you in his own way. When you wake up . . .'*

Despite her discomfiture, Betty smiled at her own silly thoughts. Maybe Barry was right about the Matheson twins. Maybe they had been playing some silly game to amuse each other. Maybe they had heard some slight movement in her cubicle and had known someone was there. They were such attractive, popular girls, their twin identities fascinating, that even if Sonia Turner, the irrascible lady captain, had been in her place, they'd have got away with their tomfoolery.

But it hadn't been tomfoolery, Betty believed, as she powdered her nose, straightened her hair and went downstairs to get supper. The girls' voices had sounded really frightened. Nothing Barry had said had altered her belief that one or other of them had somehow or other killed Gordon Rivers and that, unwittingly, she herself had been privy to a confession of murder.

Five

T en days later, the twins were having breakfast in the hotel dining room when Deborah came over to them.

'Good morning, girls!' she said, holding out two letters. 'The mail came in late this morning.' She gave a letter to each of them although both were addressed to 'The Misses R & P Matheson'. One letter had an exotic Seychelles stamp on the envelope, which she guessed was from their parents, who seemed to spend their time gallivanting around the world. Privately, Deborah disapproved of the way they neglected their offspring, allowed them so much freedom in living here at a hotel instead of in halls as did most of the first-year university students. They were not yet twenty-one – in Deborah's opinion an age which in bygone better days meant the earliest a girl should be free of parental control. The new-fangled age of maturity at eighteen was, in her opinion, far too young.

'Mine's from Ma and Papa!' Rose said as Deborah moved away. 'Who is yours from, Pops?'

For a moment Poppy did not reply. When she looked up at her twin, her face was ashen.

'What's up? What's wrong?' Rose asked as Poppy seemed either unable or unwilling to speak. Clearly her twin's letter contained bad news.

Poppy pushed aside her plate of unfinished scrambled egg and put her napkin on the table. Seeing her twin was about to leave the room, Rose did likewise and followed her into the foyer. Poppy led the way through to the conservatory,

44

which she had rightly guessed would be empty at this time of the morning when most of the guests were having breakfast.

She sat down heavily in one of the wicker two-seater sofas and Rose joined her.

'For pity's sake, Pops, what's wrong?' she repeated. 'Tell me!'

Still speechless, Poppy handed her the sheet of paper, her hand visibly trembling.

Aghast, Rose perused the contents. The words cut individually from a newspaper were stuck to a sheet of white notepaper.

£100 WILL KEEP YOUR SECRET. PUT IN WASTEBIN OUTSIDE DOOR OF DRIVING RANGE BY 10 TONIGHT.

For a moment Rose, too, was speechless. Her whole body was trembling as she put down the note and clasped the tightly folded hands of her twin. Poppy found her voice.

'Who?' she whispered. 'Who could possibly know? No one saw us!'

Rose swallowed.

'As far as we know. But someone moved the body, so someone must have been in the hotel garden late at night. Maybe . . .'

She broke off, near to tears as Poppy said: 'Is it too late for us to tell the police, Rose? I know we should have done it at the time but . . . we're being blackmailed, aren't we?'

Rose nodded.

'If a hundred pounds will keep the person from reporting us, maybe we should pay him. We can easily afford it.'

The twins' parents – who were by no means hard up – had agreed a very generous allowance for each of their daughters. When the girls had left school with reasonably good A-level results and opted to go to university, both Sir Julian and his wife, Susie, had been delighted, not wanting their freedom to sail round the world hampered by having to provide a home and occupations for their daughters. To arrange safe accommodation for them in a hotel environment, which happened also to have been their childhood home, relieved them of the anxiety most parents felt when their young daughters were launched into an adult world. Now, as they themselves were not going to be instantly available to offer help in an emergency, they had lodged a considerable amount of sterling in their English bank for the twins to withdraw on a monthly basis.

Like all their contemporaries, Rose and Poppy never missed an opportunity to buy clothes, jewellery, shoes, according to what was currently in fashion. But even so, with their hotel expenses taken care of by their father and their golf membership paid up for the year, they were hard put to use up their allowances. They had thought briefly of buying a car but neither had yet got their driving licence. As there was a half-hourly bus service from the university campus to Ferrybridge which stopped outside Ferrydene a few metres from Cheyne Manor Hotel front drive, they were happy to use this facility and save their money for the skiing holiday they intended to take the following winter.

In such circumstances, £100 did not seem too large a sum to pay. Neither would really miss £50, Poppy spoke her thoughts aloud.

'So long as whoever is blackmailing us doesn't want more,' Rose commented quietly. 'Shall we risk it, Pops?'

Poppy's face was thoughtful as she considered the alternatives. Everyone knew that blackmailers never gave up so long as the person they were robbing still had funds. On the other hand, the police inspector's sidekick had told them that the cause of Gordon Rivers' death had not yet been positively established, nor even the car identified – if car it had been – which had brought about his death. But the detective sergeant had reiterated, not without a certain amount of pride and respect, that Inspector Govern never gave up on a case where the actual cause of death and perpetrator remained unknown.

'Like the Mounties, my boss always gets his man!' DS Beck told them with his lopsided smile.

For Rose to be arrested and accused of murder – perhaps even be locked away for fifteen years – was beyond imagining, Poppy told herself now.

'We'll risk it!' she answered her twin's question with as much conviction as she could manage. 'Let's put a note inside with the money saying that it's all we've got so there would be no point asking for more.'

Rose nodded.

'He won't expect us to be rich – students never are,' she said.

Later that night, Barry Russell left the bar long enough to retrieve the envelope in the bin by the driving range. He pocketed the ten £10 notes and read the note with a chuckle. The girls could not know it, of course, but the whole idea of blackmailing them had come about through a casual remark of Betty's saying how silly the twins were to wear real silver jewellery at the club; that when they washed their hands they took off their bracelets and rings, and on several occasions she and other ladies in the changing room had had to run after them to tell them they'd left jewellery on the washbasin – the rings small enough items, perhaps, but worth at least £50 apiece. Moreover, he knew the girls had a grace-and-favour apartment at the hotel where he and Betty sometimes dined when they could afford it.

Being able to afford luxuries was certainly not the case recently for him. Two of the investments he had made with Betty's money had taken a very nasty knock on the stock exchange, and the value of his small retirement pension was nothing like as large as he had expected. Moreover, his old Honda had failed its MOT test and he'd been obliged to buy another second-hand car. Betty had refused to contribute, saying that she had run up several large bills lately, not only at the local Marks and Sparks and supermarket, but at a beauty parlour and hairdresser, and had already exceeded the monthly income from her investments.

Despite the fact that the money belonged not to him but to Betty herself, Barry had taken his wife very severely to task. In the past when he criticized her she had more often than not burst into tears and repeatedly promised to behave more economically in future. Without warning, she had suddenly stopped apologizing, and the last time he had protested about an outsize bill from Asda she had laughed in the most peculiar way and told him he'd better pay it since a husband was responsible for his wife's debts. She had also of late become extremely forgetful and he now wondered whether she was suffering from the onset of that debilitating disease, Alzheimer's. If she did go ga-ga, he told himself, he certainly wasn't going to look after her. She could go to a nursing home or wherever the state put such people nowadays.

When Betty had first told him about the conversation she had overheard in the changing room, he'd only half believed what she'd said. She was, he'd told himself, more than capable in her present mental state of having imagined the whole thing. Nevertheless, his constant need for money had prompted him to take the gamble. The twins would not know who the blackmail letter he intended writing was from, so if they were innocent they'd ignore it. The fact that they had paid up without an argument could only mean that one or other was guilty, and that his stupid wife had for once been absolutely right.

All he had to do now was to stop her from telling anyone else, and up his demands from the girls. As far as he was concerned, he couldn't have cared less about Rivers' death. He'd never liked the fellow, who rarely offered him a drink at the bar and who, when they were paired in a competition, invariably beat him.

Two weeks after his first demand for money, Barry sent a further one. This time he asked for £200. Promising each other that this would be the very last payment they made, the twins withdrew the money from their bank in Ferrybridge and put the notes in an envelope. That evening, having had supper at the hotel with John and Fred, who had stayed on after their round of golf for a meal, the four of them wandered down to the club for a drink. They stopped momentarily at the pro's shop, where Rose pretended she was interested in buying one of the new Ping putters and needed Fred and John for advice, whilst Poppy slipped across to the wastebin outside the entrance to the golf range and dropped the envelope in it.

'You should have let me do that for you,' Fred said as she returned. He was more than happy to do any small service he could for Poppy. Besides, it was almost completely dark, and after the Gordon Rivers incident everyone was nervous. John as well as Fred was being particularly solicitous, not only because of the way he felt about Rose, but because both he and Fred still felt a bit guilty about not accompanying them home on the night of Gordon Rivers' accident.

They had discussed his death quite often and reached the conclusion that neither Rose nor Poppy had been quite so bubbly, carefree or extrovert since that night. They believed that the twins were either nervous because no culprit had yet been found or worried about their recent poor exam results, both of which they denied. Whatever the reason, they did not laugh and joke and sparkle the way they used to do. Now Poppy sounded quite sharp when Fred said he should have dumped whatever rubbish she had for her – as if such a small courtesy was offensive in some way.

Fred could not possibly have known, nor indeed would he ever have guessed, that Poppy's reaction was one of horror as she imagined him seeing the sealed envelope, returning it to her in the assumption that she had dropped it by mistake, and insisting she open it to see if the contents were safe. One tiny part of her was questioning whether it might yet in the long run be the best thing to confess to what had happened. She and Rose could stop worrying, accept the consequences of the murder they – Rose – had committed and put an end to the sleepless nights and constant fear of discovery. For one thing, they need never again go down to breakfast to find another letter from their blackmailer demanding more money.

Neither she nor Rose had said as much to each other, but both were only too well aware that if the demands continued, each time for larger sums than before, by the end of the summer they would be penniless and would have to ask their father for further funds. At the very least, he would want to know how they had spent their allowances so extravagantly. Even when they were very little he had always been able to worm out of them whatever wrongdoing they had engaged in, unconvinced, as their mother had been, by their fibs and efforts to deceive him. He was the only person in the whole world they had yet come across who seemed to be able to tell one from another. It had never been of use for them to say the other was the naughty one, confusing the issue so that neither was punished. 'Punish them both!' their father had demanded, knowing that the guilty one would confess rather than have her twin suffer on her behalf.

'Well, are you both coming in for that drink?' Fred asked impatiently.

Rose nodded as John took her arm and all four went into the clubhouse. There were only four other people there: Mike Nelson, the pro, Jason Armitage and the Russells – not a very jolly group, Rose thought. As for the Russells, Barry and his wife, Betty, did not appear to be talking to each other. Betty Russell had a cup of coffee in front of her; Barry was standing up at the bar drinking whisky. Feeling sorry for the lone woman, the twins went to sit down at the table beside her. She seemed agitated as they tried to engage her in conversation whilst waiting for their drinks. Most of the time she avoided eye contact but once she stared at them both blankly as if she wasn't quite sure who they were.

Suddenly, she gave a short, nervous laugh.

'You must forgive me,' she said. 'I'm not quite myself. I think I shall go home. I didn't really want to come out this evening but . . . but Barry insisted . . .'

From his position at the bar, Barry was watching his wife's encounter with the twins. He felt profoundly uneasy. Betty was a bundle of nerves and was nearly driving him crazy with her repeated demands that he should let her tell the police what she'd heard in the changing room. This morning, to make matters a hundred times worse, she had come into his study when he was sticking on to a sheet of paper the cut-out words demanding money from the twins. She had gone completely to pieces, crying hysterically that he was a blackmailer and she would no longer keep her mouth shut now she knew his reasons for withholding the truth. He had tried to soothe her, quieten her, and finally had been forced to slap her hard across the cheek. As she had staggered backwards, she seemed to regain her composure.

'I won't keep quiet any longer!' she'd whispered. 'So you'd better stop what you are doing, Barry, else I shall tell the police about you, too.'

He'd felt a shiver of fear before it was replaced by anger. So far he had only been able to extract small sums from the Matheson twins but it was his intention to demand more and more. He'd been up to the hotel, got chatting to Pepe, the concierge, who had told him that the twins' father was a very rich and important man. '*Muchos euros,*' he had confided. Betty was not going to be allowed to kill the little geese who were laying him golden eggs. He'd have to think of some way to silence her. Run her over with a car, he thought, grinning; or, better still, get rid of her the way those girls had presumably got rid of Rivers. Not only was he sick to death of her but, as far as he was aware, she'd never made a will. Her money would all come to him when she died. *If* she died . . . *if* there was some kind of accident . . . *if* he could think of a way to make it look as if the Matheson twins had done it; *if* he could say they were paying him money to stop him telling the police he had witnessed *them* killing Betty, their motive being that *she knew they'd killed Rivers.*

These were the thoughts flitting through his alcohol-fired brain as he drove Betty home from the clubhouse in their buggy. For the time being they were more wishful thinking than genuine plans; but when they got indoors and he turned on the lights Betty was looking at him with an intensity he found unnerving.

He pulled his thoughts together, deciding that any plan to

kill her would be highly dangerous and that it must be thoroughly investigated for any possible flaw. First and foremost, he must make absolutely sure Betty was not going to the inspector to report her eavesdropping story.

'What about a Horlicks, Betts?' he suggested in a friendly tone. 'Give me a chance to think about what you were saying – about those twins and Rivers' murder.'

When she returned he took the tray from her with a rare show of good manners before saying: 'Of course, you are absolutely right to be shocked when you thought I was turning into a blackmailer. I should have explained it was an idea I had to test if the girls really had killed Gordon. If they'd paid up, we'd have known for certain that they were guilty. But perhaps it would be simpler to tell the police what you heard. It's just that I'm still afraid you'd only be held up to ridicule if you tell them the same story you told me. After all, it does sound absolutely incredible – those girls being so young. And Rivers was no weakling after all. Anyway, I've come to the conclusion that whether or not the inspector believes you, we'll have done our duty if we tell him what you heard. Then, as you say, we can sleep in peace.'

Betty made a determined effort to try to marshal her opposing thoughts. In one way, Barry's explanation could be considered plausible; on the other hand, to send a blackmail letter to the twins simply to find out if they were guilty was an extraordinary thing to do. Granted, they would not know who the note was from but if, after all, they were innocent, they might show the letter to the police, who might trace it to Barry.

But Betty wanted to believe that her husband was only acting in *her* interests; that he wanted to protect her from ridicule.

As she gathered up the mugs and put them on the tray ready to take through to the kitchen, Betty's face was a mixture of surprise, relief and a dawning pleasure. Barry was sounding like the thoughtful, caring, considerate man she had fallen in love with. Quite suddenly, he was transformed from the bad-tempered, critical, domineering man he'd been for the past few years. It was almost like having her old, dear husband back again, anxious to please her, help her, advise her, protect her, even if it was for his own benefit. Of course, in those days she'd always found ways to show her gratitude and love. Mostly those ways had been financial, which she preferred not to think about too deeply. Naturally, having no money of his own, Barry needed the help she could give him. It wasn't – as her old friend Ivy maintained – that she had to *pay* for his love.

Ivy had never liked poor Barry – not from the first day they'd met when they been out on a girlie evening together dining in the café at the end of the pier in Southdown. Barry had been fishing and had asked if he could join them at their table to enjoy his beer and a sandwich, and they'd got talking. What had upset Ivy was that he'd let Betty pay the bill because he had no money on him, he'd said.

'So how was he going to pay for himself if he'd not met up with us?' Ivy had asked as they'd walked back to their digs in Southdown. 'That man's a sponger!' But Betty had fallen instantly in love with the stranger despite the fact that Ivy had taken against him.

Maybe her money did have a little to do with Barry's consequent proposal six months later, Betty thought now. But in those days she'd all but given up hope of a husband, having reached the age of thirty-five, so she hadn't cared in the least about Ivy's warnings that it would be a mistake to marry a man younger than herself. Nor, subsequently, had she regretted that decision to accept Barry's proposal of marriage. They may have had their ups and downs, and Barry had, as the years went by, become very dictatorial, but as she said to Ivy when they still met for a cup of tea and a chat in the café on the pier, he was no different from her own father, who'd always behaved like a Victorian parent and laid down the law to his wife and family.

There had been so many compensations – at first, when Barry had been such a demanding, passionate lover; and later, when that side of their marriage had faded away, they had their love of golf in common. She'd been an exceptionally good golfer as a girl and still had a single-figure handicap when she married Barry. Still with a double-figure handicap, Barry was impressed and together they usually managed to beat their opponents when they played friendly matches. Barry was always particularly nice to her when they won.

Life had not been a bed of roses of late, however! Barry had taken to speaking to her as if she was his dog – do this, do that, fetch this, find that . . . endlessly criticizing her cooking, her driving, her clothes and, a trifle unfairly, her golf, seeing that she could usually manage to beat him when they played against one another.

Such thoughts raced through Betty's head as she bent to drop a kiss on the bald patch on top of his head. He reached up and patted her hand, nearly knocking over the tray she was now holding.

'We won't go to see the inspector tomorrow,' he said. 'I need a day or two to think what would be the best way for you to get it across to him that you're being serious. I wouldn't want him to think you were getting a bit senile in your old age.'

His smile softened his words and she sighed, saying: 'I dare say I am a bit squiffy these days, Barry – but not about this I can assure you.' Her voice had deepened into seriousness. She rested the tray on the edge of the table by the window and added: 'Do you know, I sometimes wonder if I did imagine the whole thing. And then, a minute later, I know that I didn't, although I'm as incredulous as you are about those young girls *murdering* a man like Gordon Rivers. Why on earth would they do such a thing?'

She drew a long sigh before adding: 'I know today we have girl gangs going around terrorizing and robbing people but it's for money mostly. Those Matheson girls don't need money. One of them was waving a £50 note at the bar a week or two ago and when she saw my expression, she said: "Our Papa thinks girls our age need masses of dosh to buy clothes and shoes and things so Rose and I buy most of our gear at Oxfam and only wear trainers so we have lots of spare cash for other things." "Like cigarettes!" the other twin said, "only we don't smoke," "and drugs, only we don't do pot." They were joking around, of course, but, nevertheless, they are no more the types to kill someone . . . *murder* someone, than I am.'

She looked down at Barry's impassive face.

'You're probably right, Barry, and the inspector won't believe me. If I hadn't heard them with my own ears – heard the fear in their voices – I suppose I'd have difficulty believing it.'

'Well, I shall back you up, my dear!' Barry replied as he stood up. 'Bed, I think. Now don't worry any more, Betty. In a day or two we'll have it all sorted,' he added with a little laugh.

Holding the tray awkwardly between them, Betty bent her head forward but somehow failed to plant the kiss she had intended on his lips. It would have been just a little more, Barry reflected ironically, than even his conscience could bear.

A few days later, Betty found another note demanding money in return for his silence. She had been looking for Barry's golf club diary, having mislaid her own, and in the drawer of his desk were his scissors and the seventeen words cut out of a newspaper and stuck on a plain piece of notepaper.

She went down to the sitting room and sat down heavily in an armchair, her arms and legs trembling as she realized that despite his denials and her secret fears, she really was married to a blackmiler. Barry, her husband, a blackmailer! He had never intended she should report what she'd overheard.

For all her life, Betty had tried to be a good law-abiding Christian. She upheld such principles as fairness, honesty, duty, and from time to time had had some difficulty in turning a blind eye when Barry transgressed – something which had happened all too often. Now, suddenly, it was as if a veil had been lifted and she saw him with painful clarity for what he was – the egotistical, unprincipled man Ivy believed him to be. What love she had once had for him died in that moment, and the loss of it was almost as distressing to her as the dreadful truth she had discovered – her own husband a blackmailer.

When he returned from the golf club in time for the lunch she had not cooked for him, her shock had turned to a hard, bitter anger at his betrayal.

'I hate you, Barry Russell,' she said in a cold, hard voice. 'I thought I loved you but suddenly I realize that the exact opposite is true. I hate you. I hate the way you look, talk – even the way you walk, strutting around crowing as if you were cock of the dung heap. Soon after we were married, I realized you'd only married me for my money, but I came to terms with that. Perhaps it helped knowing that however you treated me, bullied me, you could never touch my inheritance; that because you needed the money I gave you, you'd never leave me. How you resented it! Well, you can go on doing so when you have nothing else to think about whilst you're serving your term in prison for blackmail.'

She gave a strange, high-pitched laugh.

'Oh, I know I'll be punished in some way for withholding evidence about the Matheson girls, but I won't be doing time like you. I despise you and tomorrow I'm going to see Inspector Govern and I shall tell him everything – *everything*, Barry, and you can't stop me. You see, I've found that letter demanding money from the twins and I know now why you were so adamant I should not go to the police.'

Shocked beyond belief by the quiet, measured tone of this outburst, realizing that the woman meant every word she was saying, Barry collapsed into the nearest armchair. One thought now kept hammering in his brain – she'd said nothing would stop her . . . but there was something. She could have her mouth shut for ever. There *had* to be a way – some way of doing so. She stood between him and everything he had wanted. She always had; and, moreover, there was no possible way he was going to allow her to have him sent to prison. All he had to do now was to think of a safe way to bring about his wife's death.

Six

By the morning, Betty was vacillating yet again, having had most of the night to consider the consequences of her 'shopping' Barry – the publicity, her place on the golf club committee, her neighbours, friends – such few as there were. Would anyone want to partner a woman whose husband was in prison for blackmail? Golf was her one overriding pleasure in life and she could not bear the thought of having to give up the game. In short, her own self-interest was watering down her conscience. As a consequence, she would give Barry a week to make up his mind to cease his blackmailing activities and give her his most solemn promise that he would never sink to such depths of depravity again.

For seven days Barry pondered how he could kill Betty. Her discovery of Rivers' murder by the Matheson twins afforded him the perfect opportunity for getting away with *her* murder; but the question remained as to how and where. 'Where' was a fairly obvious decision, seeing that if he ever became a suspect he intended to put the blame on the twins, who, according to Betty, had already committed one murder on or near the fifth fairway. He was prepared to take a gamble on the fact that they had indeed killed Rivers – hit him over the head so it would look like a hit-and-run when they dumped him on the side of Manor Drive. Those girls would not be paying him to keep quiet if there hadn't been something pretty awful to keep quiet about, he reasoned, and if they had committed one murder, why not another?

So far he'd managed to extract nine hundred pounds from

them, but their last note enclosed with the cash was one he couldn't ignore. It said they were both overdrawn at the bank, and although they'd written to their father to ask him to authorize further funds they had no idea when their letter would reach him or even if he'd agree to do so. As far as Barry could foresee, it looked very much as if this recent source of spending money was about to dry up.

All the more reason, therefore, to despatch Betty to the hereafter, where hopefully she could chip and putt away on a Heavenly golf course to her heart's content and he would at long last have access to her inheritance to spend as he wished. But as to being the beneficiary, he would be the first suspect and his very life would depend upon him having a watertight alibi.

Sitting in his chair at breakfast, half listening to the programme on the radio, he found his concentration giving way to speculation as to how those two slim young girls had managed to get Rivers' body from the place where they had killed him. He couldn't think of a single reason *why* they should have killed Rivers in the first place; nor could he guess what any of the three of them was doing on the golf course at that time of night.

Not that it mattered, he told himself. One of the twins had murdered Rivers and got away with it – just as he intended to kill Betty and get away with it by making it look as if there was a serial killer around. Apparently Rivers had been killed by a blow on the head. Well, that would not be a problem. He could use the large adjustable spanner he had in the boot of his car. Of course, his alibi would need to be watertight. To put it mildly, too many people at the club knew he wasn't exactly an adoring husband! To be away fishing was the obvious safeguard. Sea fishing for bass was one of his main hobbies, in which he indulged once or twice a month.

There was a good beach in Southdown near the pier where several other keen fishermen would gather. To catch the night tide, one or two kipped out in their beach huts, which lined the pebbled shore. Others, like himself, took a bivouac, snatching a few hours sleep whilst waiting for the tide to turn. It had to be an incoming tide and night fishing was often as productive, if not more so, than daytime. Most of the fishermen lived in or around Southdown and would go out on to the sands a day earlier and dig lugworm for bait. There were always one or two who would let him have some. What better alibi could he have? All he needed was a method of nipping back unseen to the house to kill Betty, dump her body somewhere on or near the 5th fairway, and get back to the beach unnoticed.

'Barry! BARRY!' His wife's voice jolted him back to the present. He stared at her, wondering how he could ever have wanted to make love to her . . .

'Barry, what on earth's the matter with you? Your breakfast is getting cold. Do you or don't you want another cup of tea?'

Barry sat up in his chair, straightening his back.

'Yes, tea'll be fine!'

If she wasn't here to nag him – which she surely would – he'd have a brandy rather than tea, he thought. Maybe he would have one after she'd gone upstairs to make the beds. They slept in different rooms now – an arrangement he had been able to suggest when she complained once too often about his snoring. God, how he hated her! Just because she held the purse strings, she thought she could boss him about and she was not obliged to consider he was head of the house and his wishes paramount. That was the way it had been with his parents. Betty, damn her, argued every bloody point: 'Oh, no, Barry, I don't think we should buy a new car this year . . . No, not Scotland, Barry, it's too cold up there. I think we should go to Cyprus – to that nice hotel we were at where they had the karaoke . . . But Barry, I only bought those clubs for you last year. What makes you think you'll play any better with Calloways?'

By the time Betty returned from the kitchen with a fresh pot of tea, his hatred of her was so intense he could barely bring himself to look at her. They sat in silence until suddenly she said: 'You haven't changed your mind, Barry? You know, to stop what you've been doing? I really don't want . . . I mean I'd hate it if I had to . . . to . . .'

'Get me sent to prison?' Barry's voice was sharper than he intended. He softened it as he added: 'Of course I won't go on with it. You're absolutely right, Betty, it was a damn silly thing to do, I don't know what I was thinking about. Honestly, Betts, you have my word I won't repeat it.' He tried to make his voice sound affectionate as he added: 'And you must promise me you won't tell anyone.'

'I'm so glad, my dear.' Relaxing, she looked at him almost fondly. 'You can't imagine how worried I've been. I'll be able to get a good night's sleep now you've given me your word. It's the Ladies' Invitation match next week so I do need to be calm.' The intensity of her relief made her garrulous and she continued: 'I think I stand quite a good chance of winning this year . . . or I might if I could only improve my chipping. It seems so silly to be living on the edge of a golf course with a perfectly good driving range and never find time to practise . . .'

Her voice trailed on but Barry was no longer listening. Betty herself had solved his dilemma; shown him how to go about shutting her tiresome mouth for ever.

'You should let me help you,' he said. 'I know you don't like it when I criticize your play on the course, but I really can show you what you are doing wrong. It's such a simple little adjustment.' He paused to see if she was responding to his somewhat unusual offer of help. She was looking at him eagerly, so he went on: 'Why don't we get up early tomorrow morning or the day after? It's broad daylight by six, so we could nip down to the bottom of the garden on to the eighth and have half an hour's tuition. Personally, I can't think how Mike didn't spot what's wrong the last time you had a lesson. After all, he is the pro! Just as well I spotted the problem.'

'Oh, Barry, would you really be able to put me right? But you know we aren't allowed to get on to the course from our gardens. If—'

'If poppycock!' Barry interrupted but tempering his usual hectoring tone. 'Who on earth's going to see us at six in the morning? Even if one of the neighbours was up for some reason, they wouldn't be able to see us through those oaks and hollies and sycamores . . . proper jungle out there!'

Whilst Betty rambled on about her chipping difficulties, Barry's mind was working furiously. Yes, he could as easy as pie get on to the 8th without his neighbours seeing either of them. The 8th fairway was as good a place as any to bump her off. Moreover, it was wooded all the way round the south side of the fairway, so if he used their buggy, which he kept in a shed at the bottom of the garden, he could whip her body round in it to the 5th, leave both it and the buggy there. He'd need to prove he was somewhere else . . . The beach? Fishing? He'd need to return in the early hours and . . .

And what? he asked himself. How was he going to get back to the beach? As far as that went, how would he get back *from* the beach without being noticed? He'd need a watertight alibi – another fisherman who didn't see him leave or returning. Before he did anything else, he must check the tides.

On the following morning, Barry took Betty to the practice putting green outside the golf club. At half past eight in the morning there was nobody there. Before he allowed her even to touch a ball, he pointed out that he was in no doubt that the major fault with her chipping was that she was not keeping her head still; moreover, she was stabbing at the ball rather than following through. He took an eight iron out of her golf bag,

'But Mike uses a wedge,' Betty remarked doubtfully.

'Of course he would if the green was sloping downhill, but in my opinion you'll get a much better feel of the green with an eight iron. Moreover, I consider it's a much easier club to use than a wedge.' Barry threw two balls down six feet from the edge of the green. 'Now try that,' he said. 'And don't forget, keep your head still and hit through. Whatever you do, don't quit on it.'

Concentrating on what she had been told, on Betty's first attempt the ball rose two feet, dropped twelve feet from the pin and rolled to within a foot of the flag. She turned to look at her husband, her face glowing.

'Why ever didn't you put me right before?' she said breathlessly.

'Because you never asked me,' he replied, his voice less caustic than usual. 'Now let's see you do it again.'

There was less of a success with the next ball but nevertheless, a marked improvement was apparent by the time Barry ended his tuition half an hour later.

'You've done so well, my dear, we'll have another go tomorrow morning,' he said as they walked over to the clubhouse to have breakfast – something they had not done since playing together in a mixed foursome a long time ago.

When Betty telephoned Ivy later that day, she could not refrain from references to Barry's changed behaviour.

'I know you think he's not always as nice as he should be to me,' she said to her friend, who considered Betty's remark a gross understatement. 'And I'm not denying that's true. But he's being really, really kind lately. Do you know, he spent half an hour this morning helping me with my golf and then we had breakfast together and he's going to give me some more lessons when I want; and, Ivy, I do believe he has just been going through some kind of phase – you know, like a sort of male menopause!' She gave a shaky little laugh, aware that if she herself could believe this it would make his unmentionable lapse into blackmail a little more excusable. And it was only a lapse, she was sure. Now that he knew she knew what he'd had in mind and that she would report him, he'd be bound to reform.

'And guess what,' she added to the silent Ivy, 'Barry said I'm to invite you to dinner at the club next week – it's a gala dinner in aid of a children's hospice. You'll come, won't you? Then you'll see for yourself what a changed person Barry is.'

Barry was indeed a changed person. He was hyped up as if he'd taken drugs. He had just done a test run and proved his suspicion to be fact – he could get from the beach to the car park in just over two minutes; drive from Southdown to the field entrance leading off the back drive to Cheyne Manor Hotel in exactly nine and a half minutes. In the very early hours of the morning he might even be able to do it in eight. From there across the golf course to his back garden was four and a half minutes. Assuming Betty was up and dressed as she usually was by seven a.m., he could have her clubs strapped into the buggy and be out through the garden gate on to the 8th fairway in another five. Allow himself fifteen to kill her, drive round in the buggy to the 5th green and dump her in the approach bunker, five more to get to his parked car, ten at most to get back to the car park by Southdown Pier and two minutes to get back to his bivvy on the beach. In all, he would have been away from his fishing for fifty-three minutes.

There was insufficient time that afternoon to plan any further, or, more to the point, check on his plans. This evening he would tell Betty that he was going fishing – something that would not surprise her as he enjoyed his bass fishing at least once a fortnight. But, meanwhile, he was playing eighteen holes with Melville Sanders and needed his wits about him. Melville took his golf very seriously and usually managed to beat Barry when they paired up for a game.

That evening as he packed his new carbon fibre rod – a present from Betty last Christmas – into their Mazda, he went over his plans for what he hoped would be the last time. He took only a few of his lugworms out of the fridge, not too many, so that he'd have good reason to approach Charlie, the chap who was often as not fishing down by the pier and who was to be his alibi. Charlie would surely remember giving him some bait if he was questioned. He now put his bivouac into the boot together with his sleeping bag, ground sheet, waterproofs and tilly lamp.

As he closed the door of the car and went into supper, which Betty had just announced was ready to eat, he felt the tiniest twinge of regret. Betty was an excellent cook – and this meal he was about to enjoy was the last she would ever cook for him if all went well tonight and tomorrow. But his plan would have to be postponed if there were an abundance of fish. Any fool would know there was something odd about a fisherman deciding to take a kip whilst the fish were coming in on the tide.

Betty looked across the table at her husband, her face anxious.

'Is something wrong, Barry?' she asked. 'Is your steak tough? The butcher promised—'

'No, no, it's delicious,' Barry broke in. 'I was just thinking . . . that's to say I was thinking about tomorrow.'

Betty's face brightened.

'My lesson, you mean?' she asked. 'It really is kind of you. I feel so much more confident now. The only thing is, do you really think it's all right for us to practise on the 8th? You know they are pretty strict about us Beechwood Avenue residents cutting in from our back gardens. Don't you think it might be best to go up to the clubhouse and play off the 1st—'

'No, I certainly don't!' Berry interrupted fiercely, then, remembering his promise to himself to persuade her gently rather than bulldoze her into compliance with his plans, he modified his voice. 'We'll only be out on the course for half an hour. We agreed, didn't we, that no one in the houses could see us through the trees, and there'll certainly not be anyone on the course so early in the morning. So who's going to know? Really, Betty, much as I'd like to go along with you and ride round to the clubhouse, I will have only just got back from a night's fishing and be anxious to get some sleep.'

Betty reached her hand across the table to cover his, her face apologetic.

'I was being thoughtless. I'm so sorry, dear – and just when you are being so kind to me. Maybe I'll be quite all right in the competition if I just go out and practise on my own. I could—'

'For goodness sake, Betty, no – no way! You need me there to watch that head of yours. If you are on your own, you don't notice it and up it comes! No, of course I'll be all right – just ready for bed afterwards, that's all.'

Betty's thanks were so profuse, he very nearly told her to shut up – something he'd have readily done before he'd decided to get rid of her.

'What time will you be back from fishing?' she asked him.

Barry's voice rose a tone as he said: 'You know perfectly well I can never be sure . . .' Once again he controlled his irritation and said in a quieter voice: 'It depends on the fishing. It would be silly to leave just as they were beginning to take the bait, especially if it was quiet all night.'

'I'm sorry, Barry. I'm getting so forgetful in my old age. You must have told me that a hundred times. I'll expect you when I see you. I'll be up early as usual anyhow. As you know, I do like to get the washing out of the way early on a Monday. If I put it out . . .'

Barry stopped listening. The sun should be up shortly before six tomorrow, and although it would not yet have dried the dew on the grass, that wouldn't interfere with Betty's chipping lesson – if she ever had one. He had decided to deliver the fatal blow before they got through the trees between their garden gate and the golf course. When her body was found in the 5th bunker, although they'd soon realize she'd been killed, there'd be no reason whatever to suspect him. All he had to worry about was remembering to clean the spanner thoroughly before he put it back in his car; or, better still, he could take that back to the beach when he returned there and bury it in the sand.

He felt a shiver of excitement go through him. He was taking a terrible chance – and the consequences of being found out were unthinkable. The most dangerous part of his plan as he envisaged it was driving Betty's body from the 8th to the 5th, although he'd keep to the tree-lined perimeter and not go over the fairways. There'd be no danger getting back to his car since there would not be a soul on the footpath leading to the back drive to the hotel. But crossing the drive, getting out on to the main road . . . if he was unlucky, he might encounter the milkman. Somehow before this evening he must find out the exact time the milkman usually delivered to the hotel. It was too late now to call the depot but a phone call to the hotel might suffice. He would disguise his voice and pretend he was a local resident who wanted to intercept the milkman's float.

In the meantime, whilst Betty cleared away their plates and brought in the pudding, he could sit back and relax, knowing that all other aspects of his plan were complete.

Seven

He had about reached the point of no return, Barry thought, as he drove into the outskirts of Southdown. It was nearly midnight and a light wind blowing in from the south had lowered the day's warm temperatures. So far the fates had played into his hands, because the weather had changed and there had been no rain for the past three days. As a result, the fairways on the golf course were bone dry and footsteps would be invisible.

He turned into the avenue leading down to the sea on his left, and saw the arrow directing traffic into the entrance to the hospital on the sea front. He and Betty had both on occasions been in the Queen Mary A & E department, he with a broken wrist and Betty with a fish bone stuck in her throat! There'd been the usual long wait for attention but when eventually he'd been attended to, he had been struck by the friendly, caring nurse who looked after him. One day when he was passing the hospital, which was on the opposite side of the road to the pier, he had thought of the pretty young Australian girl, and that afternoon he'd seen her standing beside her car on the main road through Ferrydene village.

He'd recognized her at once and stopped his own car to see if she was in some kind of trouble. Her mishap turned out to be no more serious than that she had run out of petrol, so he'd driven her into Ferrybridge to a petrol station and invited her to stop and have a drink with him. But although she'd said she would really like that, she was going on night duty at eight p.m. and had to get home to put on her uniform, have a meal and drive back into Southdown, so there was no time.

Driving her back to her car, he'd learned that she worked night duties because she had a young child to care for during the day, and that she found the twelve-hour shifts exhausting.

Remembering the girl again when he had passed the hospital a week ago, he had also recalled their conversation, and now he was suddenly struck by the thought of those long night shifts. During those hours, her Fiesta was parked in the staff reserved area, and, according to her description of her hours of night duty, she wouldn't be using it again until eight in the morning. His mind raced back over the years to his school days. In the school he'd attended in Manchester, one of the older boys, called Dean, headed a gang who amused them- selves at night 'hot-wiring'. He was enormously admired by the younger boys (until he was caught and was locked up), and on one memorable occasion, because he, Barry, had been given an unusually large gift of cash from a visiting uncle, he was able to buy his way into Dean's gang for a night. He'd never forgotten the lesson he'd learned about opening locked car doors and starting up an engine without a key. All he needed was a piece of tubing . . .

One of the biggest threats to the success of his plan was the possibility that his own car might be recognized or at least identified as having been seen on the main road during the hour or so Betty was found to have been killed. The police always seemed to be able to find this out after a murder. Even though he had planned to leave his own car in the field entrance leading off the back drive to the hotel with the certainty that the milkman would not be along until much later, he had no way of knowing what other vehicles might be travelling in either direction along the main road to Southdown. It was the kind of detail the public were asked to report on the *Crimewatch* programme on television. To borrow the nurse's car would provide the perfect safeguard so long as there was no punch- card barrier to the staff car park.

Momentarily it crossed Barry's mind that he could dump the nurse's car some distance from the pier so that when she found it badly damaged in the morning and reported this to the police they would think it had been taken by kids joyriding. But it would take too long to get back on foot to the beach and time was of the essence. Better let the police suppose it to be no more than a thief, or a kid who'd been disturbed before he could drive the car away. Barry now swung his own car round into the well-lit hospital entrance. An ambulance came up behind him, sirens screaming, and branched off down the drive leading to A & E. A dark blue Audi came out of the staff car park without stopping. There was no barrier and Barry swung round and came out again, this time looking for 'his' nurse's green Fiesta. Sure enough it was there, parked neatly not too far from the entrance. Taking note of its exact position, he drove out of the car park unnoticed.

Such was Barry's excitement, his hands were trembling as he stopped by the concrete steps leading down to the stanchions supporting the pier. Lights from the promenade reached down across the pebbles but failed to illuminate the wide area of sand where he and other fishermen stashed their gear. Beneath the promenade wall was a row of twenty painted wooden beach huts. Nowadays, these fetched huge sums of money, but Charlie, the chap he usually parked next to, had owned one for the past thirty years. A chemist by profession but now retired, Charlie was able to indulge his passion for bass fishing, and, although in his late sixties, he was down on the sea shore almost every night whatever the weather. Although it was strictly prohibited, he would sometimes sleep in his hut if there was not much activity, and he could use it as shelter in really bad weather. Barry liked the man, who was a fount of knowledge about fish and tides and weather.

Setting up his bivouac, rod and other necessities on the sand, Barry went over to talk to him – his all-important alibi.

'Evening, Charlie! Tide coming in yet?' Barry asked although he had already ascertained the times of the tidal changes.

Patiently threading a large lugworm on to his hook, the older man nodded. He looked upward in the direction of the sky where a few smoke-coloured clouds were drifting across the moon.

'Could rain later!' he said, his voice laconic as always.

'Hope it doesn't!' Barry answered. 'I'm hoping for a really good catch tonight. On the other hand, I've got a tough golf match tomorrow afternoon so I may take an hour or two for a kip. Anyway, good luck!'

There was another nod and a grunt from Charlie who was now casting a line out over the top of the fourth breaker. The occasional glint of moonlight caught the white foam as the sea swept in towards the beach. The stong smell of seaweed and of tar coming from the breakwaters filled Barry's nostrils as he, too, began to cast. The pier over on his right cast long shadows across the sand. At the far end of the shoreline could be seen the flashing red danger light put there to alert shipping of the rocky outcrop jutting from the otherwise gentle curves of the beach.

In the daytime the noise from the pier was almost overpowering. Children on holiday shouted and screamed happily as they descended the helter-skelter, rode on the ghost train or the dodgems. Fat women, often in bikinis or too tight shorts, dropped ice-cream wrappers over the railings into the sea. Beer-bellied men in sleeveless singlets and baggy shorts swigged bottles of beer and eyed the bare midriffs of the young girls giggling and flirting with their shaven-headed escorts. It was only after the end of the summer holidays, when the pier was comparatively deserted, that Barry opted to fish from there rather than the beach.

He glanced at his watch. It was after four thirty and he hadn't had a bite. He looked across at Charlie and could just discern him hauling in a fish. Reeling in his line, he saw at once that his bait had gone, so he was now able to approach Charlie to say he'd forgotten to bring further supplies. Lack of concentration, he would elaborate, so that his alibi would be even more convincing. As he walked over the wet sand he knew Charlie would give him some of his bait as he always had plenty of lugworms. He would go down to the sand at low tide and dig his own bait whereas Barry usually bought his from the fishing tackle shop in the town.

'Not much doing tonight!' Charlie muttered. 'Bit too calm, I dare say!' As they both knew, there could be as many as four bass caught before the tide turned and the odd one on the ebb. Barry bent his head to look at the luminous dial of his watch. In three quarters of an hour's time he needed to be on his way home.

'Thanks for the bait,' he said. 'I'll fish a bit longer and then have a kip. A couple of hours will make all the difference to my golf later this afternoon. Maybe there'll be a bite or two when the tide turns.'

Charlie nodded. He was a quiet, reserved man who preferred his own company to that of others. Barry could be a right chatterbox, as his mother used to call his younger sister, and, though he had no reason to dislike him, he was always glad when Barry went back to his own pitch. He was not too displeased with the coddling he'd caught and, with nothing better to do that day, he was content to go on fishing until the tide had gone out.

Half an hour later, Barry reeled in his line and pitched his bivouac further up the beach out of the way of the incoming tide. Making sure that Charlie's back was towards him, he slipped quietly under the pier, and emerging the far side ran up the steps to the promenade. Passing his own parked Mazda, he crossed the main road, usually humming with traffic but more or less deserted now, and with his cap pulled down low over his forehead, he made his way behind the hospital building to the staff car park. He had a moment's anxiety as a car came suddenly out of the entrance and the driver pulled up and wound down his window.

'You all right?' he asked. 'You look a bit lost!'

'I was told to go to the X-ray department,' Barry said holding one arm in the other as he had done when he'd broken his wrist.

'You're way off the mark, old chap!' the man he now thought was a doctor said with a smile. 'It's back there on your left. See that sign? The next door to it. Sure you're okay?'

71

'Yes, thanks, I'm fine!' Barry said quickly, and started to move in the direction indicated before he could be offered a lift.

As soon as the man's car had disappeared, Barry slipped back into the car park and found the nurse's Fiesta. His heart beating rapidly, he disengaged the door lock, broke the steering lock and started the engine without difficulty. He was on the main road out of Southdown five minutes later.

Time had now become of the utmost importance. If he and Betty were too late on the golf course, there was the danger that some early player might be around and see them. He had already planned to deposit Betty's body in the deep bunker to the left of the 5th green, and he didn't want her found before he was safely back on the beach. Moreover, highly unlikely though it was, he did not want Charlie looking in his bivvy to tell him there were now decent bass to be had and finding him gone.

It was nearly five thirty as he turned left up the back drive to the hotel and then left again into the ungated entrance-way to the maize field. The crop wasn't ready to be harvested yet, or the maize high enough to conceal the car from any but a direct gaze. Closing the car door, he dipped in among the trees and, skirting the rough at the edge of the 8th fairway, went into his garden by the back gate.

Betty saw him as he walked up the path.

'I didn't hear you put the car away, Barry, or I'd have put the kettle on,' she said as he joined her in the kitchen. 'Why did you come in that way?'

Barry made a conscious effort to slow his breathing.

'Wanted to have a look at the course,' he muttered. 'Make sure no one was about. Never mind the tea, Betty. I had coffee from the Thermos before I drove back. Now let's get a move on. Have you changed your shoes?'

She looked at him in surprise.

'Well, hardly! We wouldn't want spikes on the hall carpet, now would we?'

In the past, he would have felt like hitting her when she

spoke in that mumsy voice, but now somehow he managed to keep in control.

'I'll go down and put your clubs in the buggy,' he said. 'That'll save a bit of time.'

'I'll be as quick as I can!' she replied, wishing he wouldn't hurry her. It made her inclined to panic. After all, what difference would a few minutes make here or there?

All the difference in the world, Barry would have told her as he fastened the buggy strap round her clubs, clubs she'd never get to use again, as it happened. He could nearly feel sorry for her until he remembered how he had almost had to beg her to buy the clubs he wanted for himself. 'But Barry, seven hundred pounds is an *awful* lot of money and it isn't as if your old Pings aren't as good as new . . .'

Well, in future he'd bloody well buy those Callaways and . . .

Betty came down the path towards him, the spikes on her shoes making clicking noises on the concrete surface.

'I'll drive,' he said, not wanting any argument as to when he needed to stop. It had to be before they came out from the shelter of the trees. He stopped briefly to open the garden gate and again after he'd driven through. When he dismounted a second time, Betty's voice followed him. 'Why are you stopping, Barry? Have we forgotten something?'

'Not strapped your clubs in properly,' Barry muttered as he took the heavy spanner out of the zipped compartment of the golf bag. Thankfully, Betty didn't turn to look at him as he moved forward and, standing behind her seat, lent sideways and hit her as hard as he could on the back of her head. He had anticipated she might not die instantly and, although he had begun to feel sick, he hit her a second time. Suddenly her body slumped forward in the seat, and lay still. Pulling himself together, he glanced at his watch. Six fifteen. He was behind schedule. Quickly, he removed the belt from his trousers, and pulling Betty's body upright he fastened her to the seat. Her head and shoulders still lolled forward but he had no time to do anything about it.

Turning the buggy round he drove quickly over the rough grass bordering the 8th and 7th fairways and on to the buggy path that hugged the footpath running between the golf course and the back drive of the hotel. He was not concerned about the tyre marks as he intended leaving the buggy on the 5th where it would be assumed Betty had driven it.

The sun was now fully up. Crows, pigeons and the occasional blackbird were out on the course looking for food. Otherwise, there was no sign of life. He could just see the roof of the hotel from where he had stopped by the bunker on the 5th but only a wood pigeon or crow could have seen him, he told himself reassuringly.

Breathing deeply as he glanced round to make certain no one was to be seen, he unbuckled Betty's body and lifted her out. Then, having removed his shoes, he carried her over to the bunker guarding the 5th green. She was no light weight and he was sweating heavily as he bent forward and tipped her body into it. Retracing his steps he returned to the buggy to collect her sand wedge and a golf ball, which he threw into the sand beside her.

Looking down at his handiwork, he congratulated himself on making her murder by a third person look perfectly realistic. Still in his socks, he made his way back to the buggy where he collected his shoes ready to put on when he reached the footpath. Once there, lined as it was by thick hawthorn and holly hedges, he knew he was safely over the most dangerous part of his plan.

By half past six, Barry was back in Southdown, the nurse's car safely parked with the door closed so there would be no immediate sign of damage. Once more no hospital member of staff or patient paid him the slightest attention. Five minutes later he was back on the beach, where he could see Charlie standing at the water's edge. He was almost back in his bivouac when, to his horror, he saw Charlie turn and walk towards him.

'Wondered where you'd got to. Had a good bit of fishing

just now.' Charlie's words sent an icy stroke of fear down Barry's back. Was this his alibi gone?

'Had to go off to the toilet . . . call of nature . . .' he muttered. 'Must have been something wrong with the mussels I had for dinner. Trouble up and down, if you know what I mean. Stopped feeling sick now, thank goodness.'

Charlie sighed.

'Happens!' he said, brief as always. 'Came over to tell you I caught a six pounder five minutes ago. Thought you'd want to be woken . . .'

As he wandered back to his pitch, Barry all but collapsed from the intense feeling of relief Charlie's last remark had rendered. Charlie had only been looking for him for five minutes. Before that, he'd supposed he, Barry, was asleep. His alibi was as sound as ever. He'd stay here fishing now until at least nine thirty. By then, Betty's body would most certainly have been found by the early starters. When they came to his house to report her death, he would be innocently fishing on Southdown beach, and Charlie would say that the two of them had been there all night.

Eight

It was Bob Heath, owner of the little village of Ferrydene's only taxi cab, who would be the first to see the woman's body in the bunker at the side of the 5th green. The right arm of the unfortunate corpse was stretched skywards, as if the woman had been trying to reach for a handhold on the steep sandy bank, or had, perhaps, been signalling for help.

But neither Bob nor his partner, Melville Sanders, were as yet aware of the shock awaiting them. Melville had spotted a buggy on the side of the fairway and, supposing someone was searching for a lost ball near the footpath, they were awaiting the usual courtesy wave to allow them to go through.

Melville was looking puzzled.

'Didn't see anyone going off ahead of us, did you?' he asked Bob. 'What say we play our second shots and if whoever it is emerges we'll wait till they've played?'

Bob had been about to tell his partner one of his inexhaustible repertoire of jokes. Some of them were quite funny but Melville, like any of Bob's sundry golfing partners, found them distracting, especially when concentration was of paramount importance. However, having for once driven off the tee and managed to keep his ball dead centre, Bob was quite anxious to see if he could do the same with his irons. But as usual he had sliced his next shot and his ball had soared off to the right and landed in the bunker guarding the green, whilst Melville had picked a five iron instead of a seven and his ball had flown way over the top of the flag into the rough beyond the green.

'Sorry, old chap!' Bob had said cheerfully as both men picked up their golf bags. 'Shouldn't have been spouting, should I?' With no further apology, he walked off towards his ball.

Melville paused as he heard Bob's shout; he looked over in his direction thinking, by no means for the first time, that if he could have found another partner at the last minute he wouldn't be having to put up with Bob's distractions. This time the fellow was moving from side to side at the top of the bunker pointing agitatedly down into the sand.

'What's up? Bad lie?' he called with a sigh, looking across the fairway to the little tennis ball of a man with his mop of ginger curls and somewhat bandy legs who had now dropped his sand iron and was waving frantically to Melville to hurry, one hand clamped over his mouth.

'What is it? What's wrong?' Melville asked again, his stride quickening as he gauged from Bob's frenzied gestures that it was not just his golf ball he was concerned about. Within sight now of the interior of the steep-walled bunker, he stared down at the inert body of a woman. She was lying face half buried in the sand, one trousered leg twisted beneath her, one arm reaching sideways, hand outstretched as if, in a grotesque manner, she was trying to touch Bob's golf ball. The other arm reached up as if asking for help.

'My God!' he muttered. 'That woman's dead! Who is she, Bob? Any idea?'

Bob Heath was usually to be counted upon in every circumstance to be the jovial jester, but there was only an expression of horror on his face now as he turned to look at his companion. He liked Melville, the tall good-looking bachelor who was a science teacher at Ferrybridge Comprehensive. Somewhat dandified, bordering on the effeminate, Melville was one of only a few members of Cheyne Manor Golf Club who was prepared to give him a game.

Melville was now climbing down the side of the bunker and bending to look at the dead woman's face.

'I think it's Betty Russell, Barry Russell's wife!' he said to Bob. 'You know the chap – fanatical about his golf – spends hours practising? His wife's the same – both "pot hunters"!'

Realizing he was speaking about the deceased, he took another quick look at the body before saying to his shocked companion: 'Don't think we should try to move her. She's obviously dead. Look, Bob, the Matheson twins and their partners were down on the starters' list to follow us. That could be them coming off the 4th green now. Wouldn't do to let them see this. Better go back quickly and tell them not to play this hole – any hole, in fact. No need to say why – just say you've been told to tell them. Then go and find the pro and tell him what's happened. I imagine he'll close the course – until they move the . . . the body, anyway. Hurry up, Bob!' he added sharply, seeing that the man had not yet moved.

'. . . need a doctor, an ambulance . . .' Bob muttered as he hurried away to intercept the foursome coming towards them. He took one backward look at his bag of clubs lying where he had dropped it on the edge of the bunker. There were three brand new woods in there – one of them the very latest Callaway, which had cost him an arm and a leg. The thought of an arm brought the stiffened body of Barry Russell's wife to mind and he momentarily forgot his abandoned golf clubs.

The oncoming players had stopped, the twins holding their trolleys, their partners shading their eyes against the July sunshine as they stared at the man approaching them down the centre of the fairway.

'What on earth's he doing!' Poppy Matheson remarked, flicking her dark-brown hair away from her suntanned face. 'Can't be coming back this far to look for his ball, surely!'

Her twin shrugged, her violet blue eyes, identical to her sister's, staring up the fairway. 'If it's Bob Heath – and I'm pretty sure it is – he could easily be looking for his ball. He's always losing them.' She turned to John, who was standing beside her. 'Did you know that he had the nerve to ask Poppy if she'd partner him in the mixed doubles on Wednesday?'

'He thought I was you, Rose . . .' her twin said, but broke off as Bob came within earshot.

He was half running as he approached them and called out: 'Go back! Go back, all of you . . .'

'Hey, steady on! What's got into you? *Go back*? Whatever for? We've only played three holes,' John McNaught said sharply.

Bob now reached them. Between gulps of air, he looked from one to the other, his face for once without a trace of humour.

'Melville – Melville Sanders . . . said to tell you . . . you've got to go back now.'

Fred recognized the note of hysteria in Bob's voice and put a hand on his shoulder.

'Steady on, old chap. What's up? Has there been an accident? Is Melville okay?'

'Yes, yes! An accident!' Bob gulped. 'I'm on my way back to tell the pro. Melville says Mike will close the course. Please take the girls back right away.'

'Okay, okay, we'll follow you!' John announced with a shrug of his broad shoulders. 'Come on, girls, best do as the guy says.'

As he and Fred went to pick up the balls from their four drives, neither man saw the horrified look on the twins' faces as they contemplated a serious accident on the 5th fairway, suspiciously close to the site of their own ordeal. Without clubs to carry or a trolley to pull, Bob was now hurrying ahead of them towards the clubhouse, leaving the foursome to follow him more slowly. He was still shocked by what he had seen and his legs were trembling as he went in search of Mike Nelson, the young South African professional. He was not only a plus-two handicap and a spectacular player, but he had the fair-haired good looks of a David Beckham and was, as a consequence, adored by all the female members. He was even now being propositioned by a brunette in the pro's shop, who was trying to persuade him to go swimming with her in Ferrybridge Leisure Centre on his day off.

'Sorry to butt in!' Bob said breathlessly. 'Got an urgent message for you.'

'What's that then?' Mike asked, winking at the girl.

'I can't – I mean it's sort of private . . . I mean . . . look, come outside a minute, please.'

There was something in the urgent tone of the man's voice which convinced Mike this was not one of Bob's silly jokes. Apologizing to the girl, he followed Bob out of the room.

Half an hour later there were no players on the course. They had been asked to assemble in the restaurant until further notice. They now sat talking in low tones, aware that someone had been found dead at the 5th hole and that they were shortly to be questioned by a police inspector.

Two police officers had by now driven out in buggies to the 5th green, where Melville was waiting beside the bunker. Shortly after, a doctor had also arrived, followed by an ambulance, which was now bumping its way across the fairway towards the car park outside the clubhouse. The only news that had filtered back was that there had been an accident and that it was Betty Russell who had died. Fred and John, like many others, were speculating as to what could have happened.

'Mrs Russell couldn't possibly have killed herself,' Fred said. 'I mean, if you were going to commit suicide, you'd hardly walk halfway across a golf course and lie down in a bunker to do it, would you?'

John gave a half-hearted grin.

'Sure, but maybe she had a heart attack?'

'Except we wouldn't all be shut up here and told to wait for questioning if the doc had said she'd died of natural causes. It has to have been murder! Maybe her husband wasted her. What do you think, girls?'

Poppy and Rose looked at one another and then, with identical gestures, shrugged their shoulders.

'It's anyone's guess!' Rose said, and Poppy nodded, adding: 'You could be wrong, Fred, as you were when you kept insisting that Gordon Rivers had been killed. "Accidental death", the coroner said.'

'Darned if I can see how this could have been an accident!' John broke in.

'Barry Russell isn't here. I wonder if anyone has told the poor chap that his wife has popped her clogs!' Fred muttered. 'Pity – I rather liked her, even if she was the world's worst gossip. You could always trust her to have the latest bit of scandal!'

'Shut up, Fred,' John retorted. 'A bit of respect would be preferable at a moment like this.'

The girls, he realized, were very far from being their usual sparkling selves. Like most of the women members, their voices were hushed and from time to time they glanced impatiently towards the door through which Sonia Turner, the lady captain, had informed them would come Inspector Govern and his assistant, Detective Sergeant Beck.

Poppy looked across the table at her twin.

'You realize they were the policemen who came to the hotel after Gordon Rivers died!'

Rose nodded. Aware that Poppy's voice had a note of anxiety in it, she added flippantly: 'All us residents were questioned, remember? And the sergeant was a bit of a flirt – quite dishy actually!'

'Well lay off the flirting when you see him today, Rose,' John said, his tone not altogether jocular. 'I like to think you're my date this holiday.'

Rose tossed her head, glad to have eased the tension she knew Poppy was feeling.

'I only promised I'd always be your golf partner,' she reminded him. 'Anyway, it was Poppy not me the sergeant was chatting up, wasn't it, Pops?'

Poppy smiled.

'Actually it was both of us, and—'

She broke off as the door opened and George Turner, the club captain, returned, this time accompanied by two men. The room fell silent as the three of them sat down at one of the tables and George Turner started to speak.

'For those of you who have not yet met these gentlemen, this is Detective Inspector Govern and his assistant, Detective Sergeant Beck, who I believe some of you met a few months ago when . . . when Gordon Rivers was killed. The sergeant will make a note of your names and addresses if you will kindly take it in turns to go to that table over by the window. Meanwhile, Inspector Govern wishes to talk to each of you privately in the ante-room. He will now explain why these procedures are necessary.'

Govern took a step forward.

'I think you probably all know by now that one of your members, Mrs Betty Russell, was found dead this morning in the bunker beside the 5th green.' There was an audible gasp from some of the more recent arrivals as he continued. 'Mrs Russell's death occurred some time around seven o'clock this morning.'

Another audible gasp followed this statement, followed by total silence as Inspector Govern went on.

'Her husband, Mr Russell, who I have now spoken to, assures me that it was not unusual for his wife to be out on the course practising at that early hour as she was very anxious to get her handicap down; and that sometimes he accompanied her. However, he was away last night fishing in Ferrybridge so Mrs Russell was alone when her attacker struck. Mr Russell was unable to suggest any reason why this might have happened since his wife carried no money when she was on the course and the only piece of valuable jewellery she was wearing was her Rolex watch, which has not been stolen. I am, therefore, assuming for the time being that Mrs Russell was murdered for some other reason. If anyone here can give me any idea why she should have been killed, I wish to hear it – or, indeed, of any suspicions you may have however unlikely. Formal statements will be taken later at the police station in Ferrybridge.'

There was now an audible exhalation of breath from his audience as he stopped speaking and was led by George Turner into the ante-room. As soon as Sergeant Beck had seated himself at a table at the far end of the room, the twins advanced towards him and seated themselves opposite him. At once his good-looking face broke into a smile.

'Thought I just might meet you two again,' he said. 'Poppy and Rose Matheson, if my memory serves me right. So which one are you – Poppy or Rose?'

'I'm Rose!' she replied with a smile.

'And I'm Poppy,' her twin added.

And fantastically tempting they both were in their minute pink shorts and figure-hugging pink T-shirts, David Beck told himself as he took his fountain pen out of his pocket and returned Rose's smile.

'And you both reside at Cheyne Manor Hotel, yes?'

'Temporarily, yes. Our home address is in France,' Rose replied. 'Didn't we tell you when you and the inspector came to the hotel that time when . . . when Mr Rivers died? Our parents live in Grasse.'

'We usually go home for the holidays, but this summer the parents are away so we're staying here,' Poppy volunteered.

Sergeant Beck, who had been busy taking notes, now looked up at the twins.

'Thank you, ladies. My inspector will want to ask you a few questions about the unfortunate Mrs Russell – mainly if you happen to know anything that might explain why someone would want to kill her.' As both girls looked nervously at one another, he added quickly: 'Nothing for either of you to worry about – simply if you noticed anyone unusual on the course this morning. You were out quite early, Mr Heath said.'

'Our partners have tutorials this afternoon,' Poppy told him, 'so we booked the earliest starting time we could.'

'And I need the practise,' Rose added. 'Poppy plays off a thirteen handicap but I'm a fourteen.'

'That's pretty impressive,' Beck exclaimed. 'I'm a twelve handicap and reckoned that wasn't too bad for a chap who has to work most of his days off. Like today, for instance. I was supposed to be playing at Ferrybridge golf course but that little fact cuts no ice with my inspector.'

'Is he an ogre?' Rose asked, glad to have the conversation diverted from Betty Russell's murder.

'Does he bully you?' Poppy asked almost simultaneously.

Sergeant Beck grinned.

'Actually, he's a really nice chap, even if he is a bit of a slave-driver. He's brilliant at his job. But if I keep you two here much longer, he may not be quite so agreeable. Thank you both for your time.'

He watched them as they walked away, their small, pert posteriors moving in unison and in the most provocative if unconscious manner. David Beck sighed, wondering yet again whether at some later date he might be able to further his brief acquaintance with the twins – invite them to his own golf club, perhaps. They wouldn't half cause a stir amongst his fellow members!

The girls were quickly forgotten as Bob Heath came up to the table. Sergeant Beck was aware that it was he who had discovered the body so he was not too surprised to see him mopping the sweat from his forehead as he sat down. Before he could speak – which he was clearly anxious to do – Sergeant Beck said: 'Just your full name, telephone number and address, Mr Heath. The inspector will be taking further details from you later.'

'Number fourteen, Brocken Road, Ferrydene,' Bob began and had to be slowed down as Beck wrote in his notebook Heath's postcode and telephone number. By then Bob could restrain himself no longer.

'It's only a small house, two up two down, but with a garage where I keep my taxi. My mother used to live with me – it was her house, of course – but she died two years ago so I live on my own. That's to say, I live downstairs. There's not much work going in a small village like Ferrydene so I let the two rooms upstairs to an old boy, retired sailor who's a bit handicapped – a bit deaf. But he's company for me and I like to think I bring a bit of sunshine into his life – tell him lots of jokes, you know?'

He paused briefly to draw breath. Before Beck could intervene, he continued.

'I used to be a comedian – played the clubs, you know? Not much of a living unless you were big time, so I came down here, bought the taxi and got a licence to run it.' Momentarily he smiled as he said: 'I've got a good joke for old Bill when I get home this evening. Maybe you haven't heard it. It's about the golfer who had tried for years to best his friend and one day he was about to do so when they were on the 18th green. He was about to putt out when a hearse went by so he stopped to raise his cap. When the hearse passed out of sight, he made his putt, missed it and lost the hole, so losing the match after all. "That was jolly decent of you," his friend said. "Stopping like that put you off your rhythm. If it weren't for that you'd have sunk your ball blindfold."'

For the briefest of seconds, Bob paused once more to draw breath, watching Beck's expression as he concluded. '"Ah, well!" the fellow said. "It was the least I could do. We'd been married for forty years!"'

Somehow Sergeant Beck managed a smile before saying quickly: 'No more time for jokes, I'm afraid. There are a lot more people waiting, as you can see. Thank you for your time, Mr Heath. I take it you are a member here – not a visitor?'

His question unfortunately leased a further diatribe.

'I certainly am! Took a bit of time to get in . . .' He lowered his voice. 'Chaps at the top are a pretty snobby lot, you know? Public school and all that marlarky.' His expression, which a moment ago had been humourous, was now plainly vicious – the transformation so marked that David Beck found himself making a mental note that this individual could not be judged on outward appearances. Beneath the clown façade lurked a very different streak.

However, the smile returned as Sergeant Beck gently dismissed him and the two lads, Fred Clark and John McNaught, took his place. Gradually as the morning wore on his list of club members and the occasional guest grew longer. Several were unable to hide their irritation at having their morning's golf curtailed, the unfortunate Mrs Russell's death seeming of little consequence to them.

Melville Sanders, who together with Bob Heath had

discovered the body, was not so much irritable as critical of the dead woman and her husband. A science teacher at Ferrybridge Comprehensive, he was a cold, austere man who clearly disliked any outward show of emotion. Barry Russell, he told Beck, was worse even than the unfortunate Bob Heath – a loud-mouthed fellow whose voice could invariably be heard above everyone else's in the clubhouse – even on the course. As for Betty Russell, she seemed addicted to gossiping to anyone prepared to stop and listen to her. He told Beck: 'It was enough to put you off your game if you were just about to hit your ball and you heard Betty's voice calling out: "No, Barry, it's behind the tree . . . not that one . . . the oak . . . that's it . . . over to your left . . ."'

Seeing that the unfortunate woman was not yet even in her coffin, David Beck thought the high falsetto take-off of her voice not a little unkind, but Melville Sanders was even more disparaging about the husband.

'Swears like a trooper. I've complained to the captain about it. It's "F . . . that for a shot" or "My ball's in the shit" or "Bugger me, I'm in the water." Women about, too. God knows how he ever got into the club.'

Govern, his boss, could put Melville Sanders on his list of suspects, David Beck thought as the man walked stiffly away after giving him his address and telephone number. A cold fish, if ever there was one.

The long morning wore on until, finally, Sergeant Beck was able to leave his position by the window and go in search of Inspector Govern. He found his superior in the washroom.

'I've got some good news for you, David,' he said as he dried his hands. 'Seeing it's supposed to be your day off and you missed your golf this morning, the captain has agreed to your getting nine holes in whilst I finish the interviews. Seems a chap called Jason Armitage needs a partner as most of the members have packed it in and decided to go home. The course has been reopened although the 5th is closed as forensic are still out there trying to find some clues.'

DS Beck's mouth fell open.

'Play golf? Nine holes? Now?' he queried.

Inspector Govern barely concealed a smile.

'Okay, I'm not pulling your leg.' His expression grew more serious. 'I was chatting to Mr Turner just now and he said Jason Armitage was a long-time member and knew most of the chaps fairly well. There's just a chance whilst you're playing that you can get some useful info from him – just throw in a casual question from time to time. Get my meaning?'

It was David Beck's turn to smile.

'Can't think of an assignment I'd like better,' he said. 'Do I take it that the woman's husband, Barry Russell, is out of the frame?'

Govern nodded.

'Seems so, but I still have reservations. I sent PC Jones, the Ferrydene chappie, over to Southdown where his neighbour told me he often went fishing. He broke the news to Mr Russell and brought him up to see me about ten thirty. Seemed pretty shocked, poor devil, although I gathered there wasn't a great deal of love lost between him and his wife. However, he says he's got what appears to be a watertight alibi – chap called Charlie Something-or-other who was fishing nearby. They'd been up all night so I didn't keep Mr Russell long. Anyway, he'll be coming down to the mortuary this afternoon to formally identify the body.'

'So it's "murder, suspect unknown",' Beck murmured. 'Well if you're sure it's okay with you, I'd love a game, of course; but I haven't yet taken details from the kitchen staff, groundsmen and so on. I've only done visitors and members.'

'No need!' Govern said. 'George Turner has already given me a list of employees and a copy of the rota for the day. However, when you've had your game I'd like us to go up to the hotel and see who's there. It's only four months, you know, since that fellow Rivers was killed.'

'Accidental death, though!'

Govern's expression was quizzical as he returned his sergeant's gaze.

'I'm beginning to wonder if it was "accidental". Even the

87

coroner was in some doubt and only reached his verdict when the pathologist agreed that the blow to the head and the body bruising *could* have been caused by a vehicle coming from behind; and, of course, that Rivers had been drinking fairly heavily and *could* have lurched into the road, perhaps hoping for a lift. Nevertheless, he agreed someone might have run into the chap deliberately.'

'You mean someone at the golf club saw him leave, got into their car and went after him?'

'We can't rule out that possibility. In the light of this second unexplained death, I'm beginning to have some more serious doubts.'

'If you're right, sir, it would mean we're dealing with a bloody nutcase!' Beck commented as they left the cloakroom.

'Your choice of language leaves a lot to be desired, Sergeant!' Govern said. 'Hopefully your manners are an improvement on your speech and you'll thank the captain very nicely for suggesting a quick nine holes for you. And you can thank me, too, for signing you off duty as of here and now. Now grab a sandwich and skip lunch or you won't get a lift home. I'm hoping to be away from here in another two hours at most.'

By the time Beck had paid his respects to the captain, retrieved his golf bag and shoes from the boot of the car and found his way to the first tee, Jason Armitage was waiting for him. He apologized for keeping him waiting but the fellow seemed in no great hurry and announced he was grateful to get a partner, albeit for only nine holes.

'Gather you're the police chappie's sidekick!' he said, shaking Beck's hand with a friendly smile. 'My name's Jason, by the way, and I play off a twenty handicap so you'll have to give me some shots.'

Beck enjoyed playing with the man, who he judged to be about Inspector Govern's age. During their game, which was fairly evenly matched, David was unable to extract any useful details about Jason's fellow members but he learned a lot about his companion. It seemed he'd grown up in Canada, where he had been taken by his parents as a boy. That explained his distinctive accent.

Apparently his parents had brought him on holiday to Southdown as a child, and when he decided to take early retirement from his job he chose to come back to England.

'I never married,' he told Beck as they came off the 9th green. 'But I'm quite content to live on my own. How about you?'

David Beck grinned.

'I'm always on the lookout for pretty girls but I don't think the irregular hours I have to work would be popular with a wife. Mind you, if one of those smashing twins was a little older . . .'

Jason smiled.

'Tell you what, if I wasn't the age I am, you could have one and I'd have the other!'

'You wish!' Beck rejoined as, seeing Govern on the terrace outside the clubhouse, he waved to him. He glanced at his watch and saw that it was almost two thirty. ''Fraid I won't have time for a drink,' he said to his partner. 'But I tell you what – we'll invite the twins to a game at my club in Ferrybridge. If they refuse, you and I can at least have a return game. Next time it will be my turn to beat you.'

Later, in the car driving back to Ferrybridge, he told Govern that although he had failed to get any useful clues from Jason Armitage he had much enjoyed his company.

At first, Govern did not reply. Then he said quietly: 'Don't get too close. George Turner seemed to think he's a bit of an oddball.'

'Jason Armitage?' Beck echoed. 'But why on earth . . .?'

'A bit of a loner, apparently – doesn't socialize and, apart from the golf, doesn't join in any of the club's activities.'

'Well, good luck to him!' Beck said. 'Obviously he's got better things to do!'

'Turner didn't think so; fellow never seems to have any friends – keeps himself to himself.'

Beck shrugged.

'He was perfectly friendly to me. In fact I rather liked him. Oh well, it takes all sorts.'

Inspector Govern nodded.

'We do have a more likely suspect, of course – Barry Russell. From my informal investigations this afternoon, we know one fact for certain – Russell couldn't stand his wife. According to George Turner, there was an implicit rule to avoid them partnering each other whenever possible because play practically ceased whilst they argued every stroke! "You lifted your head!" "No, I didn't!" "Yes, you did!" You know the sort of thing.'

'Sounds as if they should have bumped each other off!' Beck answered, grinning. 'As for Armitage, I couldn't have asked for a nicer partner. Straight as a die.'

'Which is what we'll be doing if you don't watch your driving. I know we're due at the mortuary at half three but I'd prefer it wasn't a permanent visit. Now turn left at the crossroads.'

'By the the Greyhound pub?' asked Beck, pretending innocence.

'Dead right!' said his boss with a grin. 'It'll have to be a quick one but I think it's high time we both had a drink!'

Nine

Wishing for the time being to avoid the golf course, with Betty Russell's murder reviving so many fears and horrid memories, on the day following the murder, the twins persuaded John and Fred to join them in a game of tennis on Cheyne Manor Hotel hard court. Although the boys were not hotel guests, Kevin Harris had virtually given them the run of the hotel, not for their benefit but to please the girls' father. He, himself, was not a snob but Dolores was, and Sir Julian Matheson's title, insignificant as it was, was sufficient to cause her to fawn on him on the few occasions he had come to the hotel. Kevin knew the twins had noticed – and giggled – about Dolores' behaviour, and that they took advantage of it by going to Dolores rather than himself on any occasion they wanted special treatment.

Now, after the continuous downpour of rain during the previous month, the students were enjoying the heatwave of late July. Having played two strenuous sets of tennis, they were stretched out on the grassy bank overlooking the court, and the conversation returned yet again to the murder.

'God knows what the 5th and 6th fairways will be like, not to mention the greens!' Fred commented. 'There are at least a dozen white-boiler-suited chaps crawling around on their hands and knees all over the place – looking for a murder weapon, I suppose!' He turned on his side, the better to enjoy the sight of Poppy's shapely sunburned legs now all but touching his own.

'Lucky for the guys it didn't rain last night,' John said, gently tapping the top of one of Rose's tennis shoes with his racquet.

He glanced at the girls, who seemed to be in silent communication with each other.

'Was Mrs Russell a friend of yours?' he asked.

Poppy and Rose spoke in unison refuting such an idea.

'Far from it!' Rose explained. 'Betty wasn't only the world's worst gossip, but she was unkind with it – never had a good word to say about anyone.'

John sat up and clasped his arms round his bony knees. Tall, fair haired, long legged, he looked very much the typical American athlete. By nature he was immensely kind hearted and such was his gentle, outgoing manner and friendliness, everyone liked him.

'I expect that's because Mrs Russell was always being bullied by that guy she was married to!' he said, Although he was doing a Masters in European history at Sussex University, he had suddenly become interested in psychology. As a consequence, he was now going through a phase of psychoanalysing everyone.

'And how do you know he bullied her, wise guy?' Fred challenged him.

'I was having a lesson a week or two ago with Mike Nelson,' John explained. 'Mr and Mrs Russell were coming up the 2nd fairway as we were waiting to drive off on the 3rd, so we were near enough to hear them. He was sounding off in a really loud voice. They were in a buggy and she was driving it. "For heaven's sake, watch what you're doing – no not there, this way, by that tree – are you completely stupid – that tree not the oak – oh, for heaven's sake, let me drive. You're enough to put anyone off their game . . . Move over . . .." That sort of thing. No wonder she takes it out on other people.' John's mimicry of Barry Russell's hectoring tone was excellent.

'Took it out on other people, you mean!' Poppy spoke for the first time. 'Let's not talk about her . . . or the murder.' She gave a slight shiver and Rose quickly put an arm round her.

'I'm not as squeamish as Pops,' she proffered. 'She has hysterics if she sees a squashed hedgehog on the road. And

I'm always the one who has to throw the spiders out of the window.'

'So *now* I know how to tell you two apart!' John said, laughing. 'Drop a dead spider on your lap, Poppy, and wait to see which one of you picks it up.'

'Shut up, you oaf!' Fred reproached him, taking the opportunity to put a comforting arm round Poppy's shoulders. 'You've just no sensitivity, have you?'

Before they could start one of their friendly scuffles, Rose got to her feet, saying: 'How about another set? Girls against boys.'

Immediately both John and Fred jumped up and reached for their tennis racquets. Poppy stood up more slowly. Fred put his arm round her shoulders again, his expression sympathetic as he said quietly: 'I'm not surprised if you're feeling a bit off – I mean, with Betty Russell being murdered not all that long after poor Mr Rivers kicked the bucket. I suppose the press are bound to get hold of yesterday's murder and rehash that hit-and-run carry-on as well. Do you think your parents will fly back to England?'

As he opened the gate and they filed on to the court, Rose said: 'I doubt if our parents will see an English paper. They email us occasionally just to make sure we're okay, but unless we told them something was wrong they'd see no point in coming back.'

'You're lucky to have such easygoing parents,' Fred said as he tossed a coin to see which pair would serve first. 'Mine are somewhat old fashioned in more ways than one. They behave as if I was still ten years old – you know, "Have you got your warm vest on, Freddie? Have you washed behind your ears?" That kind of thing, and if I don't ring every Sunday without fail, they're on the point of calling the police and reporting me a missing person!'

They all joined in the laughter and then directed their attention to the game. The four of them were nearly as proficient tennis players as golfers and they gave their attention fully to it.

Down at the police station, Inspector Govern was instructing his sergeant to drive to Cheyne Manor Hotel, reintroduce himself to Miss Deborah Cahill, have an informal chat with her and try and get a bit more information about the dead man, Gordon Rivers. Meanwhile, he said, he was going to have another word with the pathologist who did the post-mortem on Rivers and find out what he felt about the coroner's verdict – accidental death.

'I'm in serious doubt now as to whether it was a hit-and-run,' he said. 'And don't ask me to elaborate because I can't explain it.'

Sergeant Beck looked interested. From past experience, he knew how often his boss's hunches turned out to be relevant facts. Moreover, as Govern had remarked yesterday at the clubhouse, two deaths in three months in the same locality had to be suspect, albeit that it could have been coincidental. They were still awaiting the result of Mrs Russell's post-mortem, due at any moment, but there seemed little doubt that she had been killed by a blow to the head. Therefore, if Gordon Rivers had been killed deliberately, could it have been by the same person? And, if so, why? Those two deaths had occurred little more than six hundred yards apart.

Shrugging his shoulders and sighing, Beck went off to find Deborah Cahill, who, if his memory served him right, was bossy but ultra efficient. Maybe, he thought as he steered his car in the direction of Ferrydene village, he might see the intriguing identical twins at the hotel, which would more than make this somewhat tedious assignment worthwhile.

Deborah, meanwhile, was sitting in her office, regarding her boss's white, anxious face with misgivings. Since yesterday morning, when news of the murder on the golf course had reached them, he had seldom left her side. He was a bundle of nerves.

'I've just had a phone call from that police detective, Inspector Govern, I think his name is. He's sending his sergeant to see you, Deborah – just an informal visit, he said, but I don't like it. I don't like it at all. Why should he want to see you after all this time? Why not me? I asked him if I could help but he said there was no need to take up my time at this stage. All he wanted was a bit of information about Gordon Rivers' background. I thought all that business was finished after the coroner's report.'

'I'm sure it was, Mr Harris!' Deborah said soothingly. 'I expect the visit is nothing more than routine. The inspector would have come himself if it had been important, and asked to speak to you, not me. If the sergeant asks me about this . . . this horrible business yesterday, I shall tell him quite truthfully that I barely knew the unfortunate woman – Mrs Rushton, wasn't it?'

'Russell!' Kevin corrected her. He crossed the room to look out of the window, which Deborah had opened to let in the warm sunshine. From across the gardens, he could hear the shouts of the young tennis players. Lucky devils, he told himself bitterly – not a care in the world, whereas he was besieged with them. Not only was there the continuous nagging worry about their interference with Gordon Rivers' body, now there was this new murder, which could quite easily have been committed by the same perpetrator. No one knew *why* Gordon Rivers was lying at the bottom of the garden – thanks to Deb's idea to move him to the side of the road so it looked like a hit-and-run. But he and Deb knew better. Strictly speaking, he told himself, with this new murder, they should now reveal the truth to the police. Surely it was an offence to withhold evidence? He said as much now to Deborah.

'Yes, of course, Mr Harris,' she admitted, 'but we broke the law when we signed those statements at the police station saying we'd found Mr Rivers' body on the roadside. And yes, it is an offence to move a dead body. We'd be in very serious trouble if we confessed we'd actually moved it from a completely different place.'

Kevin collapsed into the chair opposite his PA, his face now a mask of anxiety.

'How serious?' he demanded.

Deborah swallowed her exasperation.

'I've absolutely no idea, Mr Harris,' she said, wondering

whether indeed it was an indictable offence; if maybe they could even be sent to prison – and then what would happen to Rusty? She looked down at the small, very overweight dog lying in a shaft of sunlight on the green carpet. Her heart jolted. The mere thought of being parted from her beloved pet was enough to cause her stomach to knot. Prison she could endure if the worst came to the worst, but to be there without Rusty, who might pine and . . .'

'Deborah, you're not listening to me. I said you must be very, very careful what you say to the sergeant. Make it clear you know nothing – nothing at all; that you're only my assistant and simply do what I tell you.'

With the greatest difficulty, Deborah managed to hide her indignation at Kevin's remark, coming as it did from someone who more often than not did what *she* told *him* was necessary whilst he floundered in indecision. But, as always, she found excuses for him. Yesterday afternoon, on hearing about Betty Russell's murder, Dolores had had hysterics. Poor Kevin had telephoned her office, begging her to ring the doctor for an emergency call-out and go up to his suite with brandy, aspirin – anything she thought might calm his unfortunate wife.

Her lips tight with disapproval, Deborah had done as he asked, knowing from past experience that Dolores' hysterics were in fact histrionics and that Dr Bisley would almost certainly be far too busy and sensible to come all the way out from Ferrybridge to see her. Kevin should not have married a Spanish woman, she told herself for the thousandth time. He'd been blinded by her beauty, if such it could be called. In Deborah's opinion the long-legged, big-busted Dolores, with her heavily mascaraed dark brown eyes and long black hair, looked more like a foreign prostitute than the respectable wife of a hotel manager. She was self-indulgent, lazy, bad tempered and invariably rude and disparaging about her, Deborah – seeing her not as a rival but as a barrier between Kevin and herself. The fact that, more often than not, Kevin put his wife's demands before his hotel duties only added to Deborah's dislike of the woman. She felt deeply sorry for Kevin, who she knew was unhappy, browbeaten as he was . . . and still, mistakenly, in love with his wife.

'Try not to worry, Mr Harris. I shall be most tactful with the police sergeant,' she said soothingly. 'Just sit here for a bit and relax. I'll get one of the girls to bring you a nice strong cup of coffee. Everything's going to be all right, you'll see!'

'Bless you, Deb!' Kevin said, sinking back into his chair and giving a deep sigh. 'I sometimes wonder where on earth I'd be without you. Rivers is our secret, only the two of us know, so we're perfectly safe as long as we don't tell anyone else.'

Such as Dolores, they thought simultaneously – Deborah with horror at the prospect and Kevin with despair. His wife would pour out her heart to absolutely anyone who would listen when she'd had a few drinks. He knew for a fact she'd told the club pro, Mike Nelson, that he, her husband, could only get it up once a week. A month or so ago, he'd been having a lesson with Mike and, somehow or other, the conversation had got on to the subject of sex. Mike had been boasting that he could perform three times a night and had then commiserated with him, Kevin, because he only just about managed once a week. Of course, the fellow had quickly realized he'd let the cat out of the bag, and, when Kevin had insisted he do so, confessed that Dolores had revealed this information after the champagne party they'd had down at the golf club last autumn to celebrate England winning the World Rugby Cup. Kevin remembered that evening vividly. Dolores, becoming steadily more drunk by the minute, had been shamelessly flirtatious with the tall, fair-haired bachelor – embarrassingly so. The fellow was a good dancer and Dolores loved to show off so they'd been partners most of the evening. If it hadn't been for Deborah hovering at his side urging him not to intervene he'd have drawn even more attention to them than already existed. No, Dolores was not to be trusted but, thank God, Deborah was.

Nevertheless, he was unable now to do as she had suggested

and relax when Pepe called her to the conservatory where DS Beck was awaiting her.

Sergeant Beck rose to his feet as the woman came into the room. She looked pale and rigid, he thought as she sat down beside him. Maybe working as PA to that drip of a manager, Harris, was a pretty dreary job – and exhausting, too. From what he could remember of the Rivers interviews, Mr Harris had continually referred to his assistant: What day? Which week? Who was at the hotel when Mr Rivers had first checked in? Miss Cahill had all the answers at her fingertips – or, rather, on the tip of her tongue; whereas Harris was tongue-tied and looked as if he was guilty of some ghastly mis-demeanour! He had even jokingly suggested to Inspector Govern that the wretched chap might have been the one to bump off Gordon Rivers because he hadn't paid his bill!

Pulling his thoughts together, Beck now gave his attention to Deborah Cahill.

'I suppose Mr Rivers was not in any kind of financial trouble, Miss Cahill?'

She looked at him as a Victorian school mistress might have regarded an impertinent pupil.

'As I have said, I have absolutely no personal knowledge of Mr Rivers' monetary position,' she said. 'He was certainly not in the habit of confiding such intimacies to me. However, he did always pay his bills promptly at the end of every month – except for last April when he was in no position to pay any bill.'

Beck concealed the smile which her remark had elicited.

'Of course not. However, presumably his estate has been cleared by now and the bill has been paid?'

'I understand probate was granted a fortnight ago – quite quickly, as it happened. Mr Rivers had only the one relative – a nephew, who came over for the funeral from New Zealand where he resides. He settled all Mr Rivers' outstanding bills before he went home.'

Sergeant Beck had met the nephew, who had called in to the police station and chatted to Inspector Govern. Not that the conversation had been in any way enlightening since it was close on twenty-two years since the fellow had last met his uncle, who'd been paying a brief visit to New Zealand. Apparently Gordon Rivers had only stayed two days with his relative and had flown back leaving his nephew little the wiser about his character, interests, likes or dislikes. Govern had assumed from the nephew's account that Rivers was a cold, aloof, insular man who was not interested in this sole surviving branch of his family.

Beck now resumed his questioning of the prim spinsterish woman sitting opposite him.

'At the inquest, you said you found Mr Rivers' body on the side of the road around midnight; that you were walking your pet dog before you went to bed?'

'Not exactly, Sergeant Beck. I had already retired when Rusty demanded to go out for a second time.'

Beck nodded.

'Wasn't that somewhat late for you to be out in the dark, Miss Cahill?'

Deborah's mouth tightened.

'It would be very remiss of me not to take Rusty out if he needed to go,' she said pointedly.

Beck cleared his throat.

'Of course, but it would be safer for you at night to remain within the hotel grounds,' he cautioned. 'Nowadays there are a lot of very undesirable people about – mentally unstable people who commit murder for no understandable reason. That is one of the reasons why my inspector was hoping you might be able to throw a little more light on Mr Rivers' background.'

Deborah now looked directly at him as she said firmly: 'I doubt I can be of further help, Sergeant. You probably know more than I do.'

'We know he was Scottish and that in his younger days he had a responsible post in a steelworks,' Beck told her. 'It's simply that no friends, colleagues, relatives – other than the nephew – seem to have surfaced since his death. The inspector was hoping a letter, something, or someone might have turned up at the hotel in recent weeks.'

There was a moment's silence before Deborah replied: 'Had there been such an occurrence, Mr Harris or I would have notified you,' she said pointedly. 'Now may I enquire, Sergeant Beck, if your inspector thinks there is any connection between Mr Rivers' accident and Mrs Russell's demise?'

Beck, who had been staring out of the window at the approaching tennis foursome – and in particular at the twins in their very short-skirted tennis dresses – now turned to look at the woman beside him. His boss had been right when he had described her as 'sharp as a needle' and highly intelligent . . . in fact, the power behind Cheyne Manor Hotel.

'I'm not privy to the inner workings of my boss's mind,' he prevaricated. 'He has certainly not said there is a connection. But now I mustn't take up any more of your valuable time, Miss Cahill – and I'm sure it is valuable. Please give my regards to Mr and Mrs Harris, and thank you for your assistance.'

Now that the sergeant was about to leave, Deborah managed a slight smile.

'I fear I haven't been of much help,' she said, following him through the doorway into the foyer. Pepe was at the reservations desk checking in two new guests and she excused herself with the apology: 'Forgive me if I don't see you out. I must attend to the new arrivals. If I can be of any help in the future, please let me know.'

As Beck went through the revolving front door, the twins and their escorts came walking towards him. The two lads were grinning.

'DS Beck, isn't it?' Fred said. 'We've just trounced the girls in two sets, six one, six love. How's that for a victory!'

'Don't boast!' John chided, tapping Fred on the head with his racquet. But he was clearly as elated as his friend. 'We only won because the girls weren't on form. They're usually almost as tough to beat as Venus and Serena,' he admitted to Beck, who was yet again struck by the twins' identical beauty.

But it wasn't beauty so much as attractiveness, he told himself as they parted company and he made his way to the car park where he'd left his car. Their noses might almost be called snub and their mouths were too large for perfection, yet the whole was riveting – sexy and innocent at the same time, not to mention their slim, girlish figures, full breasted but with long coltish legs and arms, the latter tanned to a golden brown.

Pulling himself together, Beck dragged his thoughts away from the twins and drove slowly back to Ferrybridge. Whilst he parked outside the police station he was still thinking about the Matheson twins. But as he went inside he remembered the stiff, bony, upright figure of the grey-haired, flat-chested Deborah Cahill. He came to the conclusion – as had very many before him – that life was not fair. It was as predictable that the unattractive spinster should have remained a spinster, unloved, sexually deprived, as it was predictable that eventually the twins would have lovers, husbands, children and lives that were totally fulfilled. Moreover, he told himself as he went in search of his boss, he wouldn't in the least mind being one of the fulfilling guys in the twins' lives!

Ten

It was ten minutes to midnight on the second day following Betty Russell's murder. DS Beck was sitting in the passenger seat of Inspector Govern's car, which was parked in a side street adjoining Southdown pier. Beck had been doing his best not to yawn as the time passed slowly, the hands of his watch seeming to crawl their way towards the allotted hour when his boss considered it would be reasonable to move.

'Can't see why you still think Russell's guilty, sir,' Beck had said when he was told they were going to check the time it took to drive from the pier to Barry Russell's house in Beechwood Avenue, kill a person, dump them in a bunker on the 5th green and drive back to the beach. 'That fisherman, Charlie Whatsit, gave him an alibi for the whole of the night.'

'We'll see!' had been Govern's caustic reply as he gave his full concentration to the notes he had made.

Now he nudged his sergeant into full attention.

'We'll be off in a minute,' he said. 'It's important we wait until the traffic is off the road. Russell would have had a clear run in the early hours so we don't want to get held up.' He glanced briefly down on to the beach below. The fisherman had shown him exactly where he and Barry Russell had each been standing. It hadn't been a good night according to Charlie – he'd expect to catch at least three or four fish but he'd only caught two, and as far as he knew Barry hadn't caught any. He and Barry had decided to wait for the outgoing tide and, meanwhile, as they often did, have a kip.

For the moment, Govern knew nothing about Charlie's

beach hut where night-time use was strictly prohibited, so Charlie had let the inspector assume that he, like Russell, had a bivouac.

'Can't tell you much about him!' Charlie had replied to Govern's questions. 'Comes down once or twice a week. Know his name – Barry Something. Lives up Ferrydene way near the golf course, he said. Gather he's even keener on golf than fishing. We don't talk much. When we do, it's about the fish, weather, tides and such.'

Barry Russell's alibi was a man of relatively few words who kept himself to himself, Govern told Beck, who, so far, was convinced that Barry was innocent.

'He'd be a bit of a mug admitting he didn't get on too well with his missus,' Beck said. 'Don't you agree?'

In the dark interior of the car, Govern smiled.

'You haven't thought it through, my boy. From what we've gathered from almost everyone at the golf club, Barry Russell and his wife quarrelled like crazy; he virtually browbeat her. No use his telling us they were lovey-dovey, now is it?'

'So if he did kill her why dump her in that bunker over by the footpath? Why not on the 8th, or even the 3rd. Both holes are much nearer the house.'

Govern stretched his back and sighed.

'We don't know he did kill her in their house. He might have taken her out in the buggy and killed her. Pity the SOC chaps couldn't find any proper footprints.'

'If there'd been a heavy dew that morning the groundsman would have been out whipping the greens. He might even have caught the murderer in the act!'

Govern gave another sigh.

'*If* your grandmother had had a beard, David, she'd have been your grandfather! Anyway, what do you mean "whipping the greens"? You're a golfer. Explain, please!'

Grinning cheerfully, Beck explained.

'The groundsman goes out and swipes the dew off the grass with a long flexible bamboo cane. Takes the water off the grass without damaging it.'

'An interesting but useless bit of information where this case is concerned,' Govern said dryly.

'If your theory was right, sir, and he did drive home, kill his wife and drive back again, he would have been taking a terrible risk. That main road into Southdown has to have had a car or two on it; there might have been people about . . . milkman, postman, that kind of thing. Granted that that old banger of his isn't particularly remarkable; however, it only needed one person to remember seeing it. But in spite of the enquiries our local bobbies have been making in the last twenty-four hours, not one blue car, Mazda or otherwise, has been reported.'

'I take your point, David. No need to elaborate any further. Now let us suppose I'm barking up the wrong tree, who do *you* think killed the unfortunate lady, because someone certainly did.'

Beck stole another quick glance at his watch – still another five minutes to go – and considered the question.

'Well, nearly everyone at the club has a watertight alibi, except that chap I played golf with – Armitage, Jason Armitage. He has a cottage just outside Ferrydene, not all that far from here, I believe, and his neighbour said he kept himself to himself. As far as we know, he got on all right with Barry Russell. He'd have no motive whatever that we know of for bumping off Betty Russell.'

In the darkness, Govern smiled.

'Carry on, David. You're doing well. We shall have to think about promoting you to detective inspector shortly!'

Beck grinned.

'No thank you, sir! I wouldn't want the responsibility. Anyway, that science teacher fellow, Sanders – he's someone I didn't take to, but he was back at the cottage he shares in the school grounds with two other teachers. I spoke to one of them and he said Sanders could never have got his car out of the garage that night and driven it away without him hearing. So who else? The twins? No way! That creep who runs the hotel, Harris? He wouldn't have the goldens! Gorgeous

Dolores? Capable Cahill? The golf pro? Those two students, Clark and McNaught? Sounds like Marks and Sparks, doesn't it?'

'That's enough, David,' Govern intervened. 'Sometimes I wonder if you take the crime of murder seriously enough. Perhaps the victim would have to be one of those pretty twins you're always on about for you to take a murder to heart.'

'Well, that would get to me, sir!' Beck admitted. 'Anyway, even if I'm not exactly heartbroken about Russell's wife, I am as keen as you are to catch the murderer. When you asked me to make further checks on Gordon Rivers' background, were you thinking we could have a serial killer on our hands? Same man killed Mrs Russell who killed Rivers?'

Govern shook his head.

'One victim was a man, one a woman; one a Scot, one English. I can't see a connection. Nor a motive. As you well know, it's very, very rare that there isn't one.'

'Well, money wasn't Barry Russell's motive as you thought earlier, sir. He didn't look particularly happy when we all listened to that solicitor chappie reading Mrs Russell's will. Barry only got the house and car and the few thousand pounds in her bank account. He must have known she'd bought herself a whopping annuity and lived on the proceeds.'

'Not necessarily!' Govern argued. 'It could have been her way to stop him spending her capital. It's quite normal for a person to lodge their will with their bank. Suppose Russell thought she would die intestate and killed her for her money? Suppose he was dumbfounded when he discovered the annuity died with her and he was going to have to live on his meagre pension? Maybe that's why he killed her!'

'*If* he did, sir. Isn't it time we made the trip and resolved that possibility?'

Govern lent forward and turned the key in the ignition.

'Got the time, David? So off we go!'

They reached Beechwood Avenue and parked the car on

the side of the road opposite the Russells' house. The avenue of small private houses did not run to street lamps so they remained virtually out of sight in the darkness.

'Time, David!' Govern said quietly. 'I'm Barry, going into the house, telling my wife to get dressed, put on her golf shoes, say we're going out for a game before breakfast . . .'

'No cup of tea first?' Beck asked.

'No, and keep watching the time,' Govern replied sharply. 'She's dressed and we go downstairs, out into the garden, lock the back door and walk down the path to the gate. The buggy is there with her clubs already in it. We go through the gate on to the course . . . drive towards the 5th green. No need to conceal tyre marks so cut across the 8th fairway, then 7th, bit longer to get to the 5th . . .'

Caught up in his boss's scenario, Beck broke in.

'Stop the buggy, hit her over the head with something heavy, wait till she stops breathing . . . one, two, three, four, five seconds . . . She's dead now. Dump body in bunker. Leave body, buggy, clubs and race to footpath. Sun up now. Daren't go over fairways. Follow footpath to back drive to the hotel. Keep close to trees. Into shrubs at junction with Beechwood Avenue and dive back into garden.'

'I'll wait a minute or two while he runs up the path, goes round the side of the house, up the front path and gets into his car. Now . . .'

They drove as speedily as they dared back into Southdown and pulled up once more at the pier.

'Well, how long?' Govern asked as he switched off the ignition.

'One and a half hours, give a minute or two either way.'

Govern switched on the interior car light and looked at his notes.

'Not good enough,' he said after a long pause. 'That other fisherman said they started to fish again at twenty past seven. He knew the time because that was high tide and they'd caught a fish as it was going out. They were there at least another two hours.'

'Which accounts for him being away from his home until ten o'clock the morning the body was found,' Beck said. 'Are we sure what time he gave the fishing a break and dossed down?' he asked.

Govern nodded.

'Same chap noted the time. Russell had gone across to him to ask for the loan of some bait. They'd agreed the fish weren't coming in and he'd looked at his watch, seen there was just over an hour to go before high tide, so they decided to snatch a bit of sleep. Russell would have had to make that trip in exactly fifty minutes, no more!' Inspector Govern said. 'So I'll have to concede better judgement to you, David. Obviously I was wrong.'

'So we can eliminate him now, but only thanks to your insistence on this experiment,' David Beck proffered generously, knowing only too well how his boss found it immensely difficult to admit his instincts had been wrong. Ever since those early interviews, he'd kept saying he just *knew* Barry Russell was guilty . . . that there was something about him . . . And it was very very seldom that his boss was wrong.

'Do you think we might have one of those nutcases on our hands, sir?' he asked as they drove back to the police station. 'An opportunist who sees a person on their own with no one in the vicinity and bumps them off for a thrill?'

Govern sighed.

'Really, David, your language does leave something to be desired. I'm even more certain now that we don't have a serial killer on our hands. We don't know for certain that Gordon Rivers was murdered nor have we found a motive for someone to kill him. If he was killed – and it's a big "if" – there's an almighty difference between running someone down and bludgeoning them. Think of Sutcliffe, Haig, Christie all despatched their victims in the same way.' He gave another sigh as he turned into the forecourt of the police station. 'I suppose all those murderers were before your time. I forget how young you are!'

David Beck grinned as he got out of the car and went round to open the door for his superior.

'Thirty next birthday, sir. Old enough to get married and have a couple of kids – if I could find the right girl. Think I might try my luck with one or other of those Matheson twins at Cheyne Manor.'

Govern gave his sergeant a fatherly pat on the shoulder.

'Bit out of your league, I'd have thought. They're students, aren't they? You don't want to get a reputation for cradle snatching!'

Beck gave an exaggerated sigh.

'You may be right, sir. They do have those two chaps in tow. Still, I read somewhere that some girls prefer older men, men with a bit of experience; you know what I mean?'

Govern laughed.

'Yes, I know what you mean, although I have to confess that the last time I invited a girl to have a drink with me, her reply was: "Get lost, Granddad!" However, I'm a lot older than you so maybe you'll have better luck. Day off tomorrow, David, so go and try your luck!'

The girls were preparing for bed that night. Rose wiped the cleansing cream off her face with a tissue and handed the jar to Poppy. Beneath the tan there were dark shadows under her eyes.

Poppy looked anxiously at her twin's reflection in the dressing-table mirror. Every single night since Gordon Rivers' death, Rose had had a nightmare, the same one, where she was pulling Rivers' body off her twin and realized he was dead, that she had killed him. Poppy had nightmares, too – but of the terrifying moment when she had been walking along the path and the man had sprung out of the bushes and she had realized he was going to rape her.

'Rose, do you think we should ask Dr Bisley for sleeping pills?' she said thoughtfully. 'It isn't just our tennis that's gone to pieces but our golf, too – and I'm sure it's all to do with us feeling so washed out.'

When they woke from their nightmares, their T-shirts wet with perspiration, they had to get up, change their clothes, and it was quite a while before they could even think about going back to sleep. Despite the one who'd had the nightmare always climbing back into bed with her sister, even with the comfort of their arms around each other, they continued shivering for some time, afraid to close their eyes in case they dreamed again.

Neither girl had ever been ill in the past and had only been to see their doctor once when they were overdue their tetanus boosters. Rose said now: 'Wouldn't he think it odd – both of us needing pills? He'd want to know why we weren't sleeping.'

'We could say we were worried about the exams or the Ladies' Medal Tournament; letting the club down or something . . .'

As her voice trailed into silence, Poppy said: 'We needn't *both* ask; just one of us and we could share the pills.'

Rose nodded, her eyes unhappy.

'John keeps saying I've changed; he thinks I've gone off him and I can't tell him *why* I've changed.'

Taking Poppy's compliance for granted, she climbed in beside her. Poppy shifted sideways to make more room for her.

'Fred said the same to me; said I'd lost my "sparkle"! Well, I don't see how we can be carefree, not ever again.'

'Maybe we should split up – pretend we really have gone off them. Did I tell you that police sergeant telephoned this evening and asked us to play golf with him and a friend at his club in Ferrybridge? I said we'd think about it but I can ring back and say yes, and we can tell the boys we've got other dates.'

Poppy remained silent for a few minutes. She really liked Fred; had thought they might be an item for the rest of their time at university. Rose, too, got on so well with John, it would be really, really sad if they broke up their foursome. On the other hand . . .

As so often happened between them, Rose voiced her twin's thoughts.

'Do we have any right to go on letting them believe we're

normal people? If they knew the truth . . . knew we'd killed someone . . .'

'Don't!' Rose broke in, near to tears. 'Anyway, Pops, I killed him, you didn't!'

'But I would have done it if I'd seen him on top of you and your club lying there.'

She, too, was on the point of tears. With an effort, she pulled herself together sufficiently to say in a steadier tone: 'At least that horrible blackmailer has stopped demanding any more money.'

Rose sighed.

'I know . . . but we can't be sure he won't start again. Maybe he's just waiting until we've got some more money in the bank. We did tell him we'd used up all our savings and had overdrafts.'

Whilst each girl was silent as they tried to take comfort from this small mercy, both were unhappily aware that they would never be free of the possibility of further blackmail – or not until the person died. They no longer asked each other whether, even at this late stage, they should go to the police and confess. Now, to add to their disquiet, there had been a second murder and Miss Cahill had told them in the coffee lounge that 'further enquiries' were being made about Mr Rivers' death. She had appeared quite agitated when she mentioned it and reiterated several times that these unfortunate incidents were very bad publicity for the hotel and golf club.

'We've had two newspaper reporters nosing around,' she'd said. 'You weren't here at lunch time so you wouldn't have seen them; they pretended they were ordinary visitors who had dropped by for a meal, but Pepe reported they were out in the garden taking photographs.'

The twins had been badly shaken. Photographs of what? they'd wanted to know, but Miss Cahill had not been able to tell them. Each mentally pictured the boundary wall over which they'd pushed Rivers' body into the hotel shrubbery. Would the reporters notice the broken branches of the rhododendron and holly bushes where he'd fallen?

Neither Rose nor Poppy would have imagined in their wildest dreams that Miss Cahill was as anxious as they were about the very same things. She, too, had had nightmares seeing herself and Kevin struggling in the dark across the lawn with the dead weight of the body, on to the gravel path leading to the back entrance of the hotel garage and relived the terror of the moment when they had heard the arrival of a car, seen it turn into the garage parking space where they'd been about to carry the dead man. She had discovered next day that the latecomer was only Armand, the French chef, returning from an evening with friends in Southdown. He'd been enjoying some excellent cognac – '*un peu trop*' he had confessed with a wicked smile. Deborah was well aware that he found it highly amusing to shock her – and she sometimes had difficulty in hiding the fact that she *was* shocked. As, for example, when once he had arrived back so late that he had been obliged to get Pepe out of bed to go down and let him in. Next morning he had insisted upon apologizing to Deborah for waking the household, telling her he had been with 'an adorable young man'. Had he not been such an excellent chef, Deborah would have insisted Mr Harris sack him; but good chefs were extremely hard to come by, especially for a moderately small country hotel like Cheyne Manor. She had not been able to relate the offence to Kevin, knowing that she would definitely blush most embarrassingly if she had to explain the chef's proclivities.

Upstairs in their attic suite, both girls tried to compose themselves for sleep. Deborah, too, was as wide eyed as they were. At the opposite end of the corridor, through the big mahogany door shutting off the Harrises' private suite of rooms, was the only person in the world she loved, and he was so unhappy he had actually confided in her the reason for his despair.

Half an hour before the lunch-time dinners had started, Dolores had made one of her rare visits to his office, he'd told her. For the most trivial of reasons, she had berated her poor, long-suffering husband in so loud a voice that, in her own office adjoining, Deborah had been forced to hear every word.

111

It seemed that he had failed to put enough petrol in their car so she had run out halfway to her hairdressers in Ferrybridge and missed her appointment. In a high, strident voice, she had called him as many unpleasant English names as she knew and then some more in Spanish. He had no consideration for her; she was bored not only with him but with life at the hotel. She would go back to Spain to her parents.

At this point, not the first time Deborah had overheard this particular threat, Kevin pleaded with her not to leave him; that he loved her; that he needed her. Deborah put her hands over her ears on these occasions, unable to bear the beseeching sound of his voice. If he would only stand up to his wife, she would tell herself, not permit Dolores to humiliate him! As a rule, Kevin gave no explanation for his doldrums which followed such scenes. But this afternoon he had been close to tears when he suddenly confessed that Dolores had threatened to leave him.

Somehow managing to keep her composure, Deborah had fought back the desire to put a comforting arm round his shaking shoulders and had said in soothing tones: 'Of course Mrs Harris will do no such thing! The threat was only made in the heat of the moment – upset as she was about her missed hair appointment. It's the kind of thing a lot of women might say. I dare say Mrs Harris took your unfortunate moment of forgetfulness as a sign that you did not really love her.'

Kevin had recovered his equilibrium when he sat up and met Deborah's gaze.

'Not love her? I've always adored her! How could she think such a thing. It's utterly illogical!'

'As indeed we women are,' Deborah acknowledged, ignoring the pain she felt when he spoke of his adoration for his unworthy wife.

Kevin had sighed.

'I suppose you're right, Debs, although I have to confess I've never known *you* to be illogical.' He'd drawn another long sigh, blown his nose and attempted a smile.

'I shouldn't burden you with my worries but thank you for listening – you're a great comfort to me, my dear!'

Now, as she plumped up her pillow and turned on her side, Deborah recalled that first endearment he'd ever expressed and tried not to feel glad that Dolores had unnerved him sufficiently for him to need her as a confidante – a 'dear' confidante. In a way, Gordon Rivers' murder, too, had brought them closer together. Their shared secret would always belong only to the two of them.

As she glanced at her bedside clock, Deborah decided that even if there came a point when the police actually tortured her in order to get a confession, she would die rather than reveal that secret. There was a cosmetics salesman now currently occupying Mr Rivers' room so she need no longer pass that door with an uneasy tremor. It was unfortunate, to say the least, that poor Mrs Russell had been murdered and new enquiries were being made about Mr Rivers as a consequence. Apparently it was now known that the poor woman had not died from a heart attack and a murder investigation was under way. Someone in the lounge had spoken about a serial killer. If it was thought that Mr Rivers had after all been killed by the same person, she and poor dear Mr Harris need have no further worries. Despite their having moved the body, the murderer would be caught and justice done.

Deborah slept and dreamed of Kevin actually putting his arms round her and kissing her when she told him the good news.

Eleven

September

By the end of September, Inspector Govern was no nearer solving the mystery of the two murders on Cheyne Manor golf estate. Despite his sergeant's belief that Barry Russell could not have committed his wife's murder, his own instinctive belief in the man's guilt remained unaltered. The motive he was less certain about. It was true that Russell had not stood to inherit his wife's wealth, since she had tied up her capital in an annuity. He could not, therefore, have expected to benefit from his wife's death unless he'd been unaware of what she had done. As to the method of killing her, this swung his beliefs more in favour of Beck's 'not guilty' verdict.

Why on earth choose the golf course on whose perimeter they lived to dispose of the body? As Beck said, he lived within easy reach of the English Channel. What better place to dispose of a body than in the sea at Southdown? Moreover, as Beck insisted, he could have driven further along the coast to one of the less frequented beaches and coves where he was known to go fishing on occasions.

There had to be an answer to the mystery and Govern had a niggling suspicion that it was tied up in some way with Gordon Rivers' death. The pathologist had now agreed that there was nothing about the condition of the dead man's body to prove conclusively that the injuries were caused by a truck. The height of a wing mirror of an ordinary saloon car had made such a blow to the back of Rivers' head not only unlikely but virtually impossible. Intensive enquiries had been made about the VW truck that did have a wing mirror so positioned

114

that coming from behind Rivers it could have struck the back of his head; but no such vehicle had been found in or around the neighbourhoods of Southdown, Ferrydene or Ferrybridge. Nor had one been seen anywhere near the golf club on the night of Rivers' death or in the early hours of the morning. Traffic police had suggested the truck might have been one of the many vehicles that used Blackberry Lane and Manor Drive as a short cut to the dual carriageway routing to London. Despite this, the pathologist had not excluded the possibility that the man's injuries could have come from a piece of metal. Nor did he exclude David Beck's suggestion of a golf club such as a number one driver because of the precise angle of the club head.

Cheyne Manor Golf Club had three hundred and fifty-two members. At least ninety per cent of those members, according to Beck, would have had similar drivers to the one the pathologist had mentioned.

By the time this last possibility had been arrived at, Govern was of the opinion that any scrap of forensic evidence would almost certainly have been removed from the offending club head, if such existed; nevertheless, all club members, visitors and staff who had been at the anniversary party were asked to produce their drivers for forensic testing. As Beck had remarked with a wry grin before the examination: 'You'll have a riot on your hands, sir. There'll be competitions, tournaments, matches booked, and, no matter what the reason, you aren't going to get them to relinquish their precious Pings and Taylor Mades whilst we look for evidence of a murder that may never have been committed.'

People were, however, surprisingly accommodating when they were told the reason for the request. One or two of the men protested that it was 'bloody silly' to be making such tests more than five months after Gordon Rivers' death. The ladies were less critical and DS Beck enjoyed the chance to meet up with the Matheson twins again. He teased them about the fact that, despite their twinship, they chose to play with different sized clubs. Rose maintained that Poppy was the better player partly because she always used a man's club for her drives. He was, of course, ignorant of the fact that Rose had swapped their father's driver with Poppy's when they had taken it to the cellar the morning after Gordon Rivers' murder.

When finally all the forensic tests had negative results, Govern managed to book a slot on *Crimewatch* asking if anyone knew the whereabouts of a truck or van with a wing mirror situated at least five foot five inches above the ground and which might have been in the Ferrybridge–Ferrydene area between eleven and one o'clock on the night of Gordon Rivers' death. The programme had gone out three weeks ago and nothing had been reported other than leads that were mean- ingless, such as the man who'd rung to say he knew his wife was 'having it off' with a removal man and was almost certainly using his van for the purpose and he *could* have been in the vicinity. And a woman in the east end of London who said her fourteen-year-old daughter had been seduced by the middle-aged man who sold the tickets at Southdown pier and he was certainly evil enough to commit a murder, and although he didn't own a car let alone a truck, van or lorry, he might have borrowed one!

Both Govern and Beck had been to Betty Russell's funeral, which was attended by most of the members of the golf club and, of course, her husband. Barry Russell had looked impas- sive as the coffin was lowered into the grave. He had accepted the condolences of those around him with no obvious show of grief. Beck thought if the man was guilty he would at least have pretended to be sad, if not distraught, in order to deflect suspicion. On the contrary, he had invited Sergeant Beck and Inspector Govern back to his house for refreshments. During the half hour they had spent at The Gables, Beechwood Avenue, DS Beck overheard Barry Russell telling Bob Heath that sad as it was for him to lose his wife, he would try to offset his grief by spending more time on his two hobbies, golf and fishing.

'He was blatantly glad to be rid of his wife!' Beck had commented.

For a month, Govern had Barry Russell shadowed. It was an expense he could not justify and by the end of August he'd called off his team. As it happened, a bank robbery had taken place on the east side of Ferrybridge and for the moment, Betty Russell's murder and the Rivers case were put on hold.

Barry, meanwhile, was still finding it extremely difficult to subdue the furious anger he felt towards his dead wife. He'd been forced to realize that she was by no means as stupid as he'd always thought her and, unbeknownst to him, had tied up her money so he would never get it. Bitterly he mulled over the terrible danger he'd put himself in partly in order to inherit but more urgently to stop her disclosing his black-mailing activities.

A month ago the Matheson girls were meeting his demands regularly and without argument, but suddenly they'd pleaded poverty. He knew that nearly all students were heavily in debt but it was common knowledge at the club that Sir Julian Matheson had sold Cheyne Manor and the surrounding acreage for an extremely large sum of money; that he had a luxury villa in the south of France and a sumptuous yacht to boot. As a consequence, he, Barry, had assumed the twins must surely get regular healthy handouts from their father. However, a casual question to Miss Cahill had elicited the fact that the girls' parents were currently sailing round the world and unlikely to be seeing their daughters before the end of the summer.

Barry dared not press the twins too hard. Quite a few people at the club had remarked that recently the girls seemed to have lost their sparkle as well as their golfing form. They'd failed to win the Ladies Open and failed to turn up for the Delia Thompson Trophy. Jim, the bar steward, was gossiping to Barry one night when there were not many people about and suggested one or other of the girls was having 'boy trouble'. Jim had said that when he saw the twins with their boyfriends there was none of the usual giggling and laughter which had always attended the four of them beforehand. Barry had over-heard Fred Clark saying he thought the girls were so low key because neither Rose nor Poppy had done as well in their exams as they'd hoped and were worried about their parents' attitude to their results. John McNaught, the American boy, thought they should see their doctor and get a prescription for vitamins or some such as they were both so pale and listless.

With no guarantee that they would not 'spill the beans' if they were driven to it by impossible demands, Barry had decided to stop sending the notes for the time being. After all, he comforted himself, he was not penniless. He still owned the house, unmortgaged; the car; their possessions. His golf club membership was paid up and his only other outgoings were his food and the minor sums he paid for fishing bait, golf balls, car MOTs and the thoroughly offensive council tax. His retirement pension covered these expenses and, with the money he had so far extracted from the twins, his bank balance looked reasonably healthy.

Having lost his match in the Autumn Cup Stableford Tournament, Barry decided to spend the day fishing. They were enjoying an Indian summer and the weather was sunny and without much wind. Although there would be a lot of people on Southdown pier, there were always fishermen there in the daytime hoping to catch late-season mackerel. In many ways he considered it could provide better sport than the night-time beach fishing he and Charlie enjoyed.

Having checked the tides, by midday Barry was mingling with the visitors strolling along the wooden planks of Southdown pier. Seagulls swooped, screeching and diving overhead, vying with the sound of the sea swell rushing past the stanchions below. There were fewer people halfway along the pier where some of the amusements had been supplanted by a large cafeteria. Here on the east side opposite the door into the restaurant the children's screams and noise of people's shouts and transistors were muted.

When Barry arrived one man had cast his line and was standing attentively at the rail watching his bobbing float. A second man with his young son stood to his right looking towards the cliffs jutting out into the English Channel from

Seaford. Barry moved quickly to the left, where in the far distance he glimpsed a lone car ferry moving away from the coast as it headed towards France.

For the next few minutes he was kept busy setting up his fishing tackle. He cast twice before he was satisfied and relaxed as he turned to gaze at the shoreline. The beach was a ribbon of people with multicoloured beach towels enjoying the last of the summer's sunshine. The shouts of the bathers as they dived into the waves was only just audible. He turned back to check his float but it was clear fish weren't biting as neither of his two companions were reeling in their lines.

He cast again and turned once more to look at the shore, this time through his binoculars. Although he had no need of these for the fishing, he occasionally took them with him as it was possible to pick out one or two really sexy-looking girls, bare legged and sometimes bare breasted in their skimpy bikinis. He was not sufficiently sexually motivated ever to try to pick up one of them, but he enjoyed looking.

As he swung his binoculars slowly along the beach, his fishing line was forgotten as he picked out a topless woman lying on her side facing a bronzed male companion whose arms were round her. Beside them was a child's buggy, the occupant obviously forgotten as it dug listlessly at the sand whilst the pair lay engrossed in each other. The way they were carrying on, it wouldn't be long before they were actually having sex, Barry thought, grinning.

He was about to turn away when he noticed another man sitting a little further up the beach behind the couple. He was beckoning to the toddler. After a moment's hesitation, the child tottered up the sand to where the man was now standing. Taking the child's hand, he pointed to the promenade behind him in the lee of which stood an ice-cream vendor.

Must be a relative, Barry thought as he turned once more to his rod. Yet again, there was no movement and boredom prompted him to turn his binoculars once more to the beach. As his eyes focused, he let out a loud 'Bloody hell!'

'Into something?' his neighbour called out hopefully.

Barry muttered a reply, too engrossed in what he was watching. The man was walking towards the dark shadows beneath the pier where the stanchions left the sea and were embedded in the sand. Not only was it the same man he'd seen earlier with the same toddler, but Barry was almost certain he recognized him. Surely, he thought, it was Jason Armitage from the golf club? The child seemed happy enough sucking at an ice-cream cone. Armitage was looking back towards the couple on the beach. They hadn't stirred except to move closer together. The man's hand was on the woman's waist, her face now buried in his chest, her arm lying across his naked thigh. It was obvious even at that distance that it was not the child, but sex they had on their minds.

Armitage had now reached the pier and was disappearing beneath it. Barry drew a deep breath. From the man's furtive glances, he knew instinctively that Armitage was up to no good. He'd been sitting too far away from the couple to be a friend or relative, and a stranger would have asked the woman if he could take her child for an ice-cream and a walk along the beach. And why go out of the sun into the dark shadows beneath the pier?

'Look after my rod, will you?' he asked the man next to him. 'Got to take a leak!'

When the man nodded, Barry turned and, as soon as he could, started to hurry back along the pier. People constantly got in his way – groups with linked arms and handfuls of candyfloss or with buggies; people pushing pensioners in wheelchairs. It seemed to him an age before he waved his ticket at the turnstile to indicate to the attendant that he'd be coming back.

He jumped off the pier on to the sand and once beneath the wooden floor above him, Barry was conscious of the sudden change in temperature. It was a moment or two before his eyes adjusted to the dark. Then he saw the man – it was indeed Armitage – holding the child tightly by one hand. The ice-cream had been discarded and the toddler, obviously now thoroughly frightened, was attempting to scream, presumably for its mother. Boy? Or girl? Barrie couldn't be sure. Armitage had his hand over the toddler's mouth and, unaware of Barrie's presence, he was speaking in a low, intense voice.

'Shut up, will you? Shut up and I won't hurt you. Just be quiet. I'm going to buy you a nice toy. I've lots of nice toys in my house. If you don't stop struggling I'll smack you . . . hard. Now shut up or—'

Barry's voice brought the threatening diatribe to an end.

'What the fuck are you doing, Jason? Let the child go. Now, or I'll call the police.'

His face a pale blue in the semi-darkness, Jason Armitage released his hold on the child – a boy, Barry now realized. Sensing this was his rescuer, the child stopped crying, scrambled over to Barry and clung sobbing to his leg. Barry had no particular liking for children of either sex and he and Betty had never wanted children of their own. Nevertheless, he drew the line at paedophilia – and for what other purpose had Armitage virtually kidnapped the small boy? It was an incredibly dangerous thing to have done. At any moment someone else could have walked under the pier – might still do so . . .

Armitage was staring at him, white faced.

'It isn't what you think,' he stammered. 'The boy was lost. I was only—'

'Shut up!' Barry said. 'I was watching you through my binoculars. You could go to gaol for this—'

He broke off as the ramifications of his own words hit him. Here in front of him was the perfect replacement for the Matheson twins. Jason Armitage was a strange bloke; kept himself to himself, and as far as Barry knew he had no close friends at the club. Rumour had it he had appeared suddenly from Canada where he'd spent most of his life, but no one seemed to know what he'd been doing all those years. He'd said he was an engineer, had worked on the railways.

The child was now sobbing uncontrollably and Barry said sharply: 'I'll take the kid back to its mother, say it was obviously lost and I found it. It's that or I tell the mother you took it.'

Armitage found his voice.

'No, please, don't do that! Please . . .!' his voice trailed almost to a whimper.

'I'll keep my mouth shut but you'll owe me. You understand? Now get off the beach. Do you hear me?'

With one last frightened look at Barry, Jason hurried off towards the steps leading up to the promenade. With the hint of a smile curling his lips, Barry took the crying child's hand and said: 'Now stop that noise! I'm taking you back to your mum, see?'

He decided against holding the little boy's hand lest a passer-by thought *he* had kidnapped him and told the child to follow him. His tears drying, the boy ran after Barry as he strode purposefully towards the snogging couple. The woman disentangled herself from the man's embrace as her child, now crying again, threw himself down on top of her.

'Excuse me, madam, but your son was lost. It might be a good idea to keep a closer eye on him, don't you think?' Barry said.

Torn between guilt, relief and irritation at the rebuke, the woman's mouth tightened.

'And it might be a good idea if you minded your own business!' she said, putting an arm round the small boy. Propping himself on one elbow, the man now decided to intervene.

'Come off it, babe! The guy was only trying to help. And shut up, you,' he added, turning to the child before he looked up at Barry. 'Thanks for bringing him back. Silly little sod's always wandering off. Thanks anyway.'

Barry turned and walked back to the pier, wondering briefly if he was hooked into a fish. As he waved his ticket at the attendant, he smiled. It might not be a decent-sized one he was hooked into, but he'd landed a much bigger fish than came out of the sea. If Jason Armitage didn't wish to do a long, very uncomfortable stretch at Her Majesty's pleasure, he was going to have to pay up – not just once but for a long, long time.

The identical thought was in Jason's mind as he drove

slowly back to his cottage. His hands were shaking as he clenched the driving wheel. He was in no doubt that Barry Russell intended to make him pay for his silence. It was common knowledge at the club that Barry hadn't come into any money when his wife died. He was always last to stand a round at the bar and, not least, he would spend hours looking for a lost ball or a tee peg as if he hadn't the wherewithal to buy new ones; in other words, he was hard up.

Armitage was still shaking as he nodded to his neighbour, who was washing his car. Going into his cottage, he collapsed heavily into one of his two armchairs. He must have been mad, he told himself . . . quite mad to risk being seen getting the kid to follow him when there were so many witnesses who could recognize him. On the other hand, a very crowded place could be perfect for passing unnoticed, everyone too busy about their own affairs to take notice of their neighbour. The temptation had been too great when he'd seen the boy wander away from his parents, who were paying no attention whatever to him. The unexpected opportunity had seemed too good to miss. There'd been safeguards. If the mother had seen him buying the child an ice-cream, he could have made out he was simply a lonely, kind-hearted individual who'd been unable to resist the boy's pleas to be given a cornet.

But they'd been too engrossed to notice as the toddler happily followed him towards the unfrequented shadows beneath the pier, licking his rapidly melting ice-cream. He'd not started crying or wanting to return to his mother until he, Jason, had tried to persuade him to go with him to the car.

His luck had then failed him yet again. It had failed him first disastrously in Canada, where he'd picked up a five-year-old kid off the street and kept him prisoner in his digs for over two months before some nosey busybody had reported he'd heard the child crying whilst he – Arnold Bellman as he then was – was at work. The police had been called, broken down the door and the boy was identified as one who'd gone missing two months before. He had been duly imprisoned and served ten years of hell, a lot of the time in solitary confinement as there were too many fellow inmates who chose not to spare paedophiles from any harm they could inflict.

Those years had been little short of a living nightmare – one he'd resolved never to risk again. As soon as he'd finished with his parole time and the need to report regularly to his probation officer, he'd gone to the friend of one of his fellow sex offenders who could get hold of stolen passports. He'd bought one in the name of a deceased engineer called Jason Armitage, thus leaving the police record and reputation of Arnold Bellman behind him for ever.

Roughly the same height, build, age and hair colouring as himself, Jason Armitage had no police record by which his fingerprints could identify him. He was therefore the ideal replacement for an ex-prisoner. All he, Arnold Bellman, had had to do was to get Armitage's passport renewed so that he could travel back to England from where his parents had emigrated.

Before that, however, he had one last task to perform as Arnold Bellman. Whilst he had been in prison, his mother's spinster sister, the Irish aunt he'd never met, had finally died and, having no children, had left her cottage in Sligo to him, her nephew, Arnold. The solicitor's letter informing him of the legacy had been forwarded to him in prison and the governor had permitted him to deal with the documents transferring the property to him. On his release, his first task was to pick up the deeds where they'd been lodged, signing his real name – not quite for the last time as he had decided in prison to sell the property. This done, he banked the proceeds in an international bank in the name of Jason Armitage.

With the cash from his own account, he purchased a flight ticket to England where he planned to live in or near Southdown in Sussex where he'd been taken for a seaside holiday as a young child. There was no chance that he would be recognized, but he would, he guessed, be able to fit in more unobtrusively in a familiar environment.

Southdown was very far indeed from being a wonderful centre of activity like Toronto! He'd thought the small seaside town seriously insignificant in comparison. However, it had the advantage of being nondescript and a place where in summer the tourists outweighed in number the local residents. He saw at once that he could 'disappear' in this environment, buying himself a tiny two up, two down cottage halfway between Ferrybridge and Ferrydene village. He had determined not to give way to his lust for children, and taken up golf as a hobby and a job in the environmental health department of the local council, thus establishing himself as a normal member of the community.

But as the years went by and he could guarantee his safe integration into the local society, his will to desist in his paedophile activities weakened. In the summer during week-ends and holidays the beaches stretching either side of Southdown pier were so crowded that small children becoming lost was a regular event. Twice he had risked taking the hand of a small child and tempting it with a promise of an ice-cream, leading it away from its parents and on to the pier. On neither occasion did anyone stop or question him. In each case he had lost his nerve and returned the child to within a few yards of the patch of sand where the parents were sunning themselves and drawn no attention to himself as he sat at a distance supposedly reading the newspaper as he watched the children at play. He was, he realized, tantalizing himself, but memories of his horrific experiences in prison had helped him to keep his proclivities under control.

Today, however, the readiness of the child to go with him and the total disregard of the parents had led him to believe the risk was minimal. He had told himself there were so many people about no one would notice him take the boy up to the car park, bundle him into his car and drive back to his cottage. After a while but before the crowds on the sea front dispersed towards the end of the day, he would drive him back and leave him somewhere on the promenade where the boy would be certain to be found. The children he favoured were too young to remember where he had driven them or even to give a good description of him or his car. His only danger was in the actual moment of abduction. It was the most appalling piece of bad luck that Barry should have been on the pier and seen him – something he could not have anticipated.

Now, through one moment of weakness, he'd risked everything. If it had not been for his past record, he might have taken a chance and told Barry to prove he'd tried to abduct the boy. It would have been Barry's word against his. 'The child was following me, asking for sweets . . .' he'd have said. Only Barry had heard the boy crying that he wanted his mother and him telling the kid to shut up or he'd be smacked. His past would be looked into; the fact discovered that his adopted persona, Jason Armitage, had been dead for ten years when Arnold Bellman had resurrected him! To be arrested on suspicion of kidnapping a child for sexual purposes, a first offence, was very, very different from the case of someone with a proven record for paedophilia.

Unable to quiet his perturbation, Jason poured himself a large whisky. Barry had intimated that he was not going to shop him but would be demanding something in return for his silence. Anything! he told himself despairingly and sat pondering what Barry Russell was likely to demand for his silence. His only other thought was that the murderer who killed the hapless Betty Russell should have killed her husband instead.

Twelve

October

It was the week before the university reopened for the Michaelmas term. For once, the twins were not sharing a double date with Fred and John, an arrangement the boys had suggested and to which Rose and Poppy had reluctantly agreed. Now, as John parked his car high up on the South Downs where he and Rose were quite alone, Rose's feeling of apprehension grew stronger. When John switched off the engine, for once he did not turn and put his arms round her as was his custom when they ended an evening out together.

'I need to talk to you, Rose,' he said quietly, not looking at her.

By Easter of their first year he and Fred were already half in love with the twins and had wanted them all to move into a flat together. Neither Rose nor Poppy had been anxious to do so, mostly because they knew their father would disapprove – not so much on moral grounds, for he was quite modern in his ideas, but because of the distraction this might prove from their studies. On top of this, they knew he had gone to a great deal of trouble to lease the attic suite at the hotel for them to share during their first year at university and had even paid a large portion of the rent in advance.

During the Easter break, the twins had occasionally stayed overnight at the flat the boys were renting in Ferrybridge. Although Fred was not well off and, like most other students, was heavily in debt to the bank, John had disregarded his friend's protests that if he couldn't pay his way he wouldn't share the flat, and had gone ahead and rented it in the hope that Rose, who he adored, and Poppy would eventually weaken and join them there.

'You know those girls won't be separated,' he'd pleaded with Fred. 'If you don't share the flat Poppy won't come and then Rose won't either. So you'll be doing me a favour.'

Both girls had had minor flings during their gap year but they'd been short lived. Now things had begun to take a more serious turn and they had even been thinking of asking Mr Harris if he would consider refunding part of the expenses their father had paid. Then, almost six months ago, Gordon Rivers had died. When speaking of it, which they did as seldom as possible, they never referred to the fact that he had been killed – only that he had died. Since then, despite John's and Fred's pleas, they had shelved any idea of advancing their love lives. They still stayed occasionally at the flat but there was a difference, one which John was now about to raise.

'I've brought you up here so we can talk completely privately and without interruption.' There was a slight pause during which he stared straight ahead of him. Then he said: 'You know I'm in love with you, Rose. It isn't just the sex thing, although that was fine, too, until . . . well, until last April when suddenly you seemed to cool off. What's happened, honey? Don't you care about me any more? Is there someone else?'

Rose covered her mouth with her hand, stifling the tiny gasp she feared was about to escape. Her heart was beating painfully in her chest and her throat was constricted with tears. Every fibre of her being longed to say: 'I love you, too, John. I'd even started to think that maybe one day . . .' But now that day could never come, and since she could no more tell John the true reason why, any more than Poppy could tell Fred, she was going to have to pretend to John that she didn't care; didn't love him. If he knew she had killed someone – was a murderess – he'd want to put as much distance between them as he could. So she could say nothing; must let matters stay as they were and allow John to go on hoping that one day she might discover she did love him; or she could break off the relationship now before it became infrangible.

When she remained silent, John turned suddenly and took hold of her arms, forcing her to look at him.

'Tell me the truth, Rose. Something has gone very wrong. Fred says he's noticed a change in Poppy, too . . . a cooling off. It's as if you feel you've got to keep me at arm's length. But why, honey? I guess you didn't mean things to get serious, is that it? You were just having a good time and didn't want things to get too heavy? It was as long ago as Easter that I realized I was in love with you. I've tried not to let you see just how serious I am because I could feel you keeping me at arm's length – metaphorically, of course. You still let me make love to you but it's not the same. I feel as if you want me to love you but won't let yourself love me. Please talk to me, honey. *Is there someone else?*'

'No, no, there's no one else!' Rose cried out impulsively, and immediately wished she'd lied and told John he did have a rival. That would have made him back off . . . and however unhappy that would make her, at least it would be kinder to him.

'Then what's wrong, Rose?'

He spoke so forcibly he sounded almost angry. Not daring to look at him, she tried to slow her breathing. Now, after nearly six months, she was trapped. Now that he had confronted her, demanded an explanation, she could no longer go on hiding behind an outward show of casual affection. Each time he made love to her, she had had to use every ounce of self-control to keep from abandoning herself to his loving. Now, when she finally had to admit to herself that she must soon lose him for ever, she realized that she was far, far more than fond of him. She loved him. And if the terrible circumstances had been otherwise and he'd spoken of marriage one day when they'd got their degrees, she would have said yes without hesitation.

'Nothing's wrong!' she lied. 'I just don't want things to get too heavy. I mean, I know you think you love me and . . . well, all four of us love each other, don't we? I know Pops adores you and I'm tremendously fond of Fred. I mean, everything's fine the way it is, isn't it?'

John released his grip on her arms and wound down the car window. Had he not given up smoking for good when he'd left high school, he'd have had a cigarette now to steady his nerves. Unusually for him, he felt completely out of his depth. Rose was talking as if she were a naive schoolgirl; as if all she wanted was 'to have some fun' and he and Fred had been conveniently to hand. It had never been like that with him. When he'd first caught sight of her and Poppy in the lecture hall he'd been unable to take his eyes off them. Gradually, as he and Fred had got to know the girls, he'd been able to distinguish between them, anyway eighty per cent of the time.

Rose was the more serious of the two – only fractionally – but Poppy was more giggly, more daredevil. She was good for Fred, who tended to be shy and more reserved than himself. Rose was completely unlike his former American girlfriends, more serene, more feminine, less assertive. He sensed that she 'mothered' Poppy and had, on one occasion, imagined her as the perfect mother for his children. He'd even gone so far as to write to his mom and tell her he'd met the girl he wanted to marry and that as soon as he could he'd bring her home to meet all his folks, who'd be sure to love her as much as he did.

Now he wondered just how premature he'd been. If Rose was speaking the truth – and he was by no means certain that she was – he'd mistaken her passionate reponses to his love-making, her sweet, intimate smiles and gentle, impulsive caresses for much more than she'd intended. Even on those occasions when he'd risked a quick 'Love you!', she'd said: 'Love you, too!', but now it would seem she hadn't really meant it. Maybe he was jumping the gun – it was after all no more than a year since they'd met. His declaration had possibly frightened her if she wasn't ready to think more seriously about their relationship. As far as he knew, Fred had said nothing as yet to Poppy, who he was far from sure was in love with him.

The twins were English girls, he reminded himself. They

weren't as experienced as the girls back home, who started boy–girl relationships when they were mere kids. Rose and Poppy had gone to a girls' convent boarding school and it wasn't until they'd been set free to enjoy their gap year that they'd started dating boys, finding out about them in person instead of from books and films and television. Back in the south of France in their school holidays they'd met one or two boys, sons of friends of their parents, but their mother had not allowed them to go to discos or places where they might have been picked up. There'd be time enough for 'all that', as she put it, when they were eighteen. Poppy had related to them one evening how she had had a crush on the Italian gardener and Rose had had a crush on one of the waiters in the restaurant her parents frequented! Both had been kissed by a randy uncle who was on leave from the French Foreign Legion and had, therefore, an aura of mystery and romance. They'd snogged boys after parties and, once or twice, things had got a bit out of hand; but neither girl had had an affair let alone a steady relationship.

Now things were different, Rose thought miserably. She really, really liked John. Sometimes at night she'd lie awake imagining what it might be like if she married him; if they'd have children; where they'd live; if John really was going to write books or teach history as a career; whether she would get along with his parents, his friends, his kid sister. For the first time in her life, she did not share her thoughts with Poppy, whose relationship with Fred was far more casual. He and her twin were almost like brother and sister, laughing, joking, enjoying each other's company and only now and again getting a little more physical. With her and John, things were much more intense and sometimes, when he was making love to her, he would say he loved her.

'You are my beautiful English rose,' he'd whisper in the darkness, 'and I love you to bits!'

Tears stung Rose's eyes at the memory. How quickly that love would turn to horror if he ever found out she had actually killed a man. Although she had hit Mr Rivers as hard as she could simply to stop him hurting Poppy, it was still murder. So far, because by some strange miracle his body had been moved to Manor Drive where Miss Cahill had found it, she and Poppy had not come under any suspicion. But it was in the lap of the gods as to if or when that unknown person might confess to what they'd done. Neither she nor Poppy could ever rest in peace. As Poppy had said only last night, 'Murderers can be discovered and put in prison years and years later. I don't think we'll ever be safe, Rose!'

Someone – the person who had been blackmailing them – knew they'd killed Gordon Rivers. Maybe he was the person who had moved the body just so they would not be found out and would therefore be ripe for blackmailing. Whoever he was, he could betray them at any time, so because of that awful secret it would not be fair of her to marry someone she loved.

'I guess I shouldn't have taken things quite so seriously,' John said suddenly, his voice tight but not quite concealing the hurt behind the words. 'Forget what I said, Rose. We'll stay friends, eh?'

Rose bit her lip.

'Well, yes, it would be best. You see, Poppy and I may not stay on and finish our course. Papa wanted us to go to the university in Nice but that would have meant we'd be living with our aunt and we wanted to be on our own. So Papa compromised and said we could live in Cheyne Manor Hotel where we'd have to behave circumspectly – not get into drugs or shack up with a penniless immigrant or something. I mean, he behaved as if we were still schoolgirls. But although we've had a lot of fun and met some really nice people – and university's fun, too – we both miss our friends – friends we made when we moved to France – French mostly . . .'

She broke off, knowing that she was floundering. Telling lies was completely foreign to her and to be sitting here in the dark, pretending to John who she loved that he really meant very little to her, was all but impossible.

He made it easier. Having listened in silence, he now said: 'You don't have to dot all the i's and cross the t's, Rose. Just answer me one thing, are you in love with one of these French guys? Is that it?'

'Oh, no!' Rose said quickly, and a moment later wished she hadn't as John once more put his hands on her shoulders and turned her to face him.

'Then if you're not in love with anyone else, there's still hope for me. Of course, I shall miss you like crazy if you and Poppy do go back to France – if that's what you both really want to do. I suppose things haven't been all that pleasant what with Gordon Rivers' accident and then poor Mrs Russell being bumped off in that macabre way. Everyone seems to think Mr Russell did it but the cops can't prove it. Was your father worried about you and Poppy, Rose?'

Rose nodded, unable to tell a further lie. As far as she knew, her parents were still completely unaware of events at the golf club. They should be home from their round-the-world cruise by the New Year and it was Poppy's idea that they should circumvent them coming to England at all by being at home to meet them. The less they knew about Gordon Rivers the better. Their mother, for one, knew their voices well enough to recognize if they trembled or hesitated when his name was spoken.

John was still holding her, his face close to hers as he said softly: 'You'll let Fred and me come and visit you, Rose?' The question hung between them. 'Your parents wouldn't look on me as a "penniless immigrant", would they?'

Despite the tears in her eyes, Rose smiled. Not daring to speak, she shook her head.

'Then I guess I'd better take you home now,' he said. 'I do seem inclined to let things get heavy, don't I? But that needn't stop us kissing . . .'

As his lips touched hers, Rose closed her eyes, wishing more than anything in the whole world that she could wipe out these last six months and be back in their former happy, carefree relationship; that they were back in the flat, in each other's arms, laughing, feeling, kissing – and, above all else, loving one another.

'I'd like to go home now, please,' she said.

Thirteen

November

For the next couple of months, Jason Armitage made spasmodic payments to his blackmailer as soon as the demands arrived – usually by word of mouth when the two of them met in the clubhouse bar and there was no one else around. Barry would see Jason sitting up at the bar and slip on to the stool beside him.

'A couple of hundred would come in handy if that's okay with you,' he'd say without preamble, and then continue in the same tone of voice with a casual remark such as: 'Slow today, wasn't it? Four and a half hours, I'd say!' Or else: 'I went fishing last night and caught a couple of really big ones – bass. I was fishing off the beach by Southdown pier.'

He'd ignore the stony expression on Jason's face and to the man's disgust, offer to buy him a drink.

'We must do eighteen together one of these days. Let me know when you'd like a game.'

Anyone within earshot would have assumed the two men had developed a friendship, but behind his impassive expression Jason's emotions were in turmoil. He was the mouse and Barry the cat . . . toying with him . . . goading him into a rash rebuttal, knowing perfectly well that he dare not antagonize his persecutor. However unlikely it was that the police would pursue any report of his behaviour that Barry might make, for there had been no witnesses, they would almost certainly make checks. It was true he had changed his name, had a valid passport and had been living a blameless life, but his fingerprints would still identify him as Arnold Bellman, paedophile, former

135

prison inmate of a Canadian gaol with two past offences taken into consideration. He'd been lucky that the other fifteen transgressions had not come to light when he'd been sentenced. The fact was he had grown careless after getting away with offences for so many years, just as he had become not only careless but downright stupid that day on the beach when Barry had seen him. He'd ignored the chances of his being recognized.

When Barry Russell made his fifth demand – double the amount of the previous payment – Jason knew that somehow it had to stop. Ever since he had seen a programme on television about kids on some Far Eastern island queueing up to sell themselves to foreign male visitors, he'd realized that this was where he must go to live. There'd be no danger there where such a way of life was commonplace, and although he'd have to pay for his pleasures, it wouldn't be much and he'd travel out there with enough money to see to his needs for the forseeable future.

Sitting in his cottage staring at his latest bank statement, Jason saw that what had once been a very healthy balance on the credit side was now steadily going down, despite the fact that he lived very frugally and paid over half his salary into a savings account. He'd arrived in England virtually penniless but with his stolen British passport had had no difficulty in establishing his right to work. Moreover, although there'd been a shortage of available jobs in Ferrybridge, he'd quickly found employment in Southdown. It was not his intention to stay in England for more than a few years – until he'd saved sufficient money to guarantee him the kind of life in the Far East that he craved.

He'd been able to control his sexual urges just the way he'd been obliged to do in prison. The temptation was there, of course, the stronger for having been denied for so long. But he'd vowed he would never go back to prison, where most of the time he had been in fear if not actually of his life then of being seriously physically hurt. Single-mindedly, he pursued the dream that had kept him going during his long confinement – of a country where kids as young as four or five would be available whenever he felt the need.

Now he faced the fact that something had to be done if his dream was still to be realized. He toyed with the idea of trying to move somewhere where Barry Russell couldn't find him – Ireland, France, Australia ... but he'd learned enough in prison to know that a man's whereabouts could always be traced even if it took a long time to do so. And if he did prove too difficult to locate, Barry could shop him and he'd be back to square one.

There was only one easy way to stop a blackmailer, his cellmate, Starky Cox, had told him, and that was to 'waste him'. Doing fifteen years for manslaughter, Starky was an authority on killing. His advice on getting rid of an enemy was: 'Blast him! If you haven't got a blower, drown him! And if you can't do that, string 'im up.' He would then perform a little demonstration. 'See this?' he would say to his circle of admirers, holding an imaginary wasp between his thumb and index finger. 'Wants to sting me, doesn't it?' Then he'd hold out his arm at shoulder height, drop the invisible wasp and stamp on it. He had no need to add: 'Won't sting me now.' His audience had got the message.

So, would it be as simple as Starky maintained? Jason asked himself. He had no gun. If he bought one, it could be traced to him. Drowning? He could hardly expect Barry to agree to go boating with him. Poison him? He deserved it but, again, poison could be traced to him. No, he'd lost too many years of his life already without risking the loss of the few he had left.

Whilst he continued to meet Barry's ongoing demands, placing them in the bin by the golf range, he became ever more determined to 'waste' Russell, as Starky would have said. There had to be a way. Strangling, smothering were briefly on his list of possible methods but were rejected on the grounds that Barry was undoubtedly stronger than himself. Sticking a knife in him might result in he himself being splattered with droplets which he couldn't see but which could be detected by forensics. For all he knew, the Canadian prison service had not only got his fingerprints but a DNA sample, too.

He lay awake at night wondering if there might be some way he could tamper with Barry's car; but how to do so without being seen was an insurmountable problem since the car was either in Barry's garage or in the golf club car park in full view of any golfer who happened to be there. There just *had* to be a way, but for the present Jason couldn't think of it.

Barry was enjoying himself. When he saw the Matheson twins in the clubhouse, he made a point of greeting them with remarks that had a double meaning. 'You two look as if you haven't a care in the world, but why should girls like you have anything to worry about, I ask myself?' Or, even more upsetting for them, he said: 'Do you know, when I was playing the 5th hole with Sanders this morning, I could have sworn I saw someone trespassing. Melville said I was imagining things, but . . . well, maybe I was.'

Suspecting that he might be their blackmailer, the girls did their best to keep away from him but it was not always possible. John and Fred liked to have a beer at the end of a game and it would have seemed very strange if they refused to join them in the bar. If Barry was there, he'd approach the four of them, ostensibly to ask about their play but inevitably he'd say something meaningful to the twins.

'Did you watch *Midsomer Murders* last night?' Or: 'I'm standing the next round; I suspect being students you girls are probably hard up?'

The latter remark had been questioned by John after Barry had departed. Rose and Poppy jumped in with different explanations – Poppy saying they were in the pro's shop when she asked Mike if she could owe him for a box of new balls as she hadn't any money on her; whilst Rose said: 'He saw me looking at one of the new putters, which I said was too expensive for me to buy.'

As they had spoken simultaneously, each was equally

flustered – a fact which John noted, but he refrained from commenting. Neither twin had ever mentioned their family's financial situation but he had assumed they must be well off, living as they did in a villa in the south of France and swanning round the world on their private yacht. Maybe they'd suddenly become impoverished and that was why Rose had told him she and Poppy might go back to France to complete their degrees. As for himself, he had inherited a tidy sum from his late grandmother and, on top of that, his father had insisted he have a very healthy allowance whilst he was in Europe. If the twins were short of money, he could well afford to help them out but he knew they would be embarrassed if not offended were he to offer to do so. Fred was the same, which was why he scaled down his own expenditure, so that Fred could cope on a fifty-fifty basis as he would never have agreed to John picking up the tabs.

Barry, meanwhile, had begun to feel he could relax. It was now four months since Betty's death and that detective fellow seemed to have abandoned hope of finding whoever'd killed her. He'd had an uncomfortable few weeks when Govern and his assistant were nosing round his garage, garden, buggy shed, not to mention the house. He'd even seen them pacing the distance between his home and the bunker where Betty had been found. Not that he'd ever really feared detection. Charlie had told him the police had questioned him and that he'd left them in no doubt that Barry was fishing with him that night and early morning. According to Charlie, they'd been making enquiries about Barry's car – whether anyone had seen it leave the car park during the night. Charlie had looked quite shocked when Barry told him the police obviously suspected him of murdering his wife. With so much publicity locally about her body being found on the golf course, he'd wanted to know if Barry was thinking of moving away.

Barry denied any such possibility.

'I've no intention of being intimidated!' he said. 'After all, I'm innocent. Why should I have to upheave myself? Besides,

I'm as anxious as the police are to find the murderer. There are a lot of funny people around these days.'

Whilst Charlie was nodding his agreement before returning to his base where his two fishing lines sat on their tripods, Barry smiled as he baited his own hook. One of those 'funny' people was Jason Armitage. Ten to one he'd been up to mischief walking away with that kid on the beach. The fellow wouldn't have paid up so quickly if he hadn't been caught at it before now; maybe had a record; maybe had even done time. Whatever, Armitage was now regularly putting a couple of hundred pounds in the wastebin by the golf range and he, Barry, was seriously thinking of doubling the amount. But having wrung the girls dry doing just that, he resolved to temper his demands.

So far, the handover of the money had gone without a hitch. The bins were emptied at seven a.m. on a Monday morning, and he'd pretend to throw in some rubbish when he drove into the car park at nine to collect the money Armitage had left at eight thirty. Armitage wasn't at all keen on this arrangement. He'd agreed it would be too dangerous to hand the money directly to Barry in the clubhouse or on the course. They could never guarantee they would be unobserved. Armitage had suggested he take the money to Barry's house but Barry suspected he might still be under some kind of police surveillance and they might report these weekly visits – the more dubious as the two men were known to be anything but buddies in the clubhouse.

Jason was far from approving his blackmailer's choice of depository. He was by no means the only person who might be in the car park at eight thirty in the morning. The greenkeeper and his assistant, for two; the three female cleaners from the agency; a delivery van bringing drinks, food, groceries; not to mention the pro, Mike Nelson. Not least, there could be a number of golfers anxious to make an early start and get home in time for lunch. Anyone going to the wastebin immediately after they'd seen him depositing rubbish might well catch sight of the brown envelope containing the ten £10 notes.

He must think of a better, safer place, he told himself as he went off to play a round with Bob Heath. Whatever the cost, he must keep Barry's mouth shut for the present.

As he and Bob Heath walked up the fairway of the 2nd hole, Bob was in one of his jocular moods, most often adopted when he was in the company of someone he considered superior to himself. Not only did Jason have a much lower handicap than himself but he was obviously from a much better educational background. He himself had no regular golfing partners and relied on Mike pairing him up with some other single player – someone whose partner had cancelled at the last minute, perhaps; or a lone visitor to the course.

Now, as they took their second shots to the green, Bob shanked his three iron and his ball went flying into the lake lying between this fairway and the 1st. Two moorhens flew off screeching and there was a flurry of water as the ball fell amongst the large carp who'd been basking in the shallows.

'Bad luck, Bob!' Jason said automatically as his own ball went soaring up and over the bunker on to the green. Far from rolling towards the flag, however, it appeared to shoot off at right angles and come to a stop.

'Something on the green!' Bob remarked as he put down another ball and played it up near to his partner's.

As the two men approached, both stopped and stared. A line of freshly erupted molehills crossed the left-hand side of the green and disappeared into the hedge bordering the gardens of the houses at the top end of Beechwood Avenue.

'Greenkeeper can't have been out this morning!' Jason muttered as he regarded the not insignificant damage. 'He'll have something to say about this little lot!'

Bob shrugged.

'Wouldn't have happened overnight,' he said, and pointed to the hedge. 'That's where the little blighters come from. There must have been a few molehills coming from there before this lot. Joe will blow his nut! And it's the Ladies' Team Trophy tomorrow. I'd like to see Madame Captain's face when she sees this.'

Jason picked up his ball and placed it to one side, equidistant from the hole. Like Bob, he could imagine the expression on the greenkeeper's face. Molehills on the fairway were not unusual round the less wooded areas of the golf club, and there'd been an outbreak in the rough between the houses and the 3rd fairway; but Joe seemed to know how to get rid of them and, so far, none of his precious greens had succumbed.

Bob was grinning.

'What's the betting he'll blame these "newfangled" methods of getting rid of moles,' he said as he followed Jason's example and repositioned his ball. '"Give me me old traps any day of the week!" he said last time he had trouble. But George Turner said it took too long to catch them all and they weren't as certain to do the job effectively as the poison gas. You just stick a cartridge down the main run and the gas spreads to all the other runs, according to Joe.'

'An osmotic holocaust!' Jason said as he knocked his ball into the hole.

Not understanding the words and feeling at a disadvantage, Bob resorted to one of his jokes.

'Heard the one about the mole who went into the pub and asked for a pint of beer?' he said to Jason as they walked towards the 3rd tee. Not waiting for an answer, he elaborated: '"That'll be five quid," the barman said. Not knowing the true price, the mole went and sat down at a table. Presently he was joined by a man who looked at him curiously and said: "Don't often see a mole in a pub drinking beer." "Should think not," said the mole, "not with beer at five quid a pint!"'

But Jason had not heard this paltry piece of humour. His mind had been focused exclusively on one single thought – poison cartridges which killed moles must surely, in sufficient quantities, kill a man?

Fourteen

Kevin Harris was a bundle of nerves. Time was running out and he could no longer postpone what must be the worst task he had ever undertaken. He must give Deborah Cahill notice. With only three weeks to go before Cheyne Manor Hotel and Golf Club were taken over by the Leisure Times Conglomerate, she would have every right to be angry with him.

As Kevin closed the door of his office and sat down at his desk, he looked unhappily out of the window. Heavy dark grey clouds forecast yet another day of rain. The trees in the garden were bare of leaves and the flower beds looked neglected despite the efforts of a full-time gardener. Maybe this was the best time to be leaving, he tried to comfort himself – before the spring when everything looked bright and sunny and welcoming.

Ever since Dolores had insisted he sell to Leisure Sports, he had wondered whether it was the right thing to be doing; whether, as Dolores insisted, she really would be happier living in Brighton, where at least something happened. She was 'bored, bored, bored to the death' here in this wet, boring village of Ferrydene. The amount of money offered by the conglomerate for the hotel was '*magnífico*'. They could afford to buy a club which would be far more '*divertido*'. Far more entertaining for whom? he had asked her. Was it Dolores' intention to act as a hostess in this hypothetical club?

Surprisingly, Dolores, who seldom left the hotel, went out on her own to Brighton and found not only a club but a really nice house not ten minutes' drive away – both of which could be bought and still leave a great deal of money in the bank for holidays, clothes, the newest TVR sports car for her and, if he wanted it, a Porsche for him.

Kevin broke off his reverie to glance at his watch. Any moment now, Deborah would call in to discuss the day's business. There was plenty to do and part of the deal with Leisure Times was that everything would continue to run smoothly until the handover. They had agreed to honour the Matheson twins' tenancy agreement so there was no need for the moment to tell them about the takeover. Deborah was another matter . . .

Deborah made her way to Kevin's office in a far happier frame of mind than she had been in throughout the past two months. For some reason she had been quite unable to fathom, Kevin had excluded her from meetings he had had with two gentlemen in suits who spoke with quite marked Liverpudlian accents, and were making regular visits to the hotel. They were down south on business, they had told her, but did not disclose what their business was. Both played golf and spent quite a lot of time at the golf club. When she had asked Kevin about them, he had told her that they were property developers hoping to take advantage of the buoyant housing market in and around Southdown. The men seemed well mannered, paid their bills promptly and tipped the staff well, so were acceptable residents. They'd left a week or two ago.

It was not their presence that she had found upsetting but the fact that, for the first time since she could remember, Kevin had excluded her from his office when he'd been talking to the visitors. He had always relied on her to have the necessary information in her head when visitors wanted to know names of theatres, times of buses, where to hire a boat and so on. 'Miss Cahill will help you,' he'd say. 'She's a positive fount of information and I sometimes wonder where on earth we'd all be without her!' She treasured these moments of praise – the more so because she knew he really did rely on her. His memory was by no means very good, poor dear, and

Dead Centre

Deborah suspected that his 'cruel' wife undermined his self-confidence with her constant criticism.

Now the men had left, Christmas and the New Year were behind them and she was busy planning the special menus for the arrival of a large golf society in a fortnight's time. Mr Harris, dear man, seemed in a far happier mood. When his wife did come looking for him, for once it was with a bright smile and an entirely different tone to her voice – as if their relationship had taken a sudden turn for the better. As Pepe had remarked, Mr Harris looked far less tense these days and even smiled from time to time.

Kevin, however, was not smiling as she went into his office and sat down in her usual chair opposite him. He merely grunted a greeting and then bent his balding head to shuffle some papers on the blotter in front of him.

After a moment, he looked up and briefly met her gaze.

'You've been with me for a long time, Debbie – close on thirty years, I believe . . .'

Deborah smiled.

'Thirty-two years next month!' she corrected him.

Kevin did not return her smile but picked up a pen and began doodling on the blotter.

'Yes, well, I can't tell you how much I have valued your . . . your services . . . expertise . . . everything, really. I want you to know how grateful I am . . .' He broke off, and seeing that Deborah was gazing at him uncomprehendingly he continued desperately: 'Things won't be the same without you!'

Deborah's eyes widened in utter disbelief.

'Without me? I don't understand. You aren't *retiring*, are you, Mr Harris?'

It was the only possible reason she could think of where he might no longer need her assistance.

'No, no, of course not!' He gave a nervous little laugh. 'I'm only fifty, you know. It's just that . . . well, I suppose I should have told you before but we've sold the hotel and golf club.'

Only momentarily silenced by the look of utter astonishment

145

on the face of the woman opposite him, he added: 'We're moving to Brighton.'

Two things struck Deborah in the brief silence that followed Kevin's announcement: first, that this move must have been his wife's idea. Second, that he was obviously finding it difficult to talk about the proposed move because he thought he was going to lose her.

'Oh, Mr Harris, you should indeed have told me before and saved yourself the worry,' she said urgently. 'Of course I'll come with you. Brighton is only half an hour's drive away. In any event, I expect you'll be wanting me to live in. You've bought another hotel, have you not?'

Kevin turned away in dismay when he heard her words. Now he looked up at her expectant face and despaired.

'Well, no, not actually! We've bought a little club . . . in one of those narrow roads between the Lanes and the railway station . . . and Dolores has found a house for us not too far away, so you see . . .'

Despite her initial shock and disappointment, Deborah still did not fully grasp what Kevin was finding it so difficult to tell her.

'Then I shall have to commute, won't I? That's if I remain here in Ferrydene or Ferrybridge. I dare say if I put my mind to it, I could find a narrow flat in Brighton. I'd often thought that one day, when you no longer needed me and I finally retired, I might go to Brighton. There's the Pavillion and the Theatre Royal and that lovely big promenade which goes all the way to Hove – such a nice respectable part of—'

'Deborah!' Kevin's voice was almost shrill as he interrupted her, unable as he was to hear any more of her hopes for the future. He made an effort and lowered it as he added huskily: 'Deborah, I'm really very sorry about this but I won't be able to continue employing you. My wife thinks we should have much younger staff at the club and . . . well, I suppose it isn't all that far off your retirement anyway, is it? Of course, I will ensure you get good redundancy pay and you've your pension to look forward to and . . .'

'You're sacking me?' Deborah's voice was little more than a whisper.

Fearing she might be close to tears to add to his immense feeling of guilt, he said anxiously: 'Please don't think of it like that, Debbie, my dear. It really isn't a dismissal. It's just that there won't be a suitable job for you where we're going. Personally, I shall miss you quite dreadfully. No one could have looked after me better than you have. I wish . . . I wish . . .'

Horrified by the agonized expression on Deborah's face, his voice failed him altogether. This was, of course, Dolores' doing.

'You're not taking that old *bruja* with you, Kevin,' she'd stormed at him. 'I won't have it. What do you think the young people who come to these clubs would think when they seed her? Perhaps it wouldn't matter quite so important if she was attractive, chic, *elegante* – someone her age who looked like Joan Collins. But not *her*. Besides, it makes me feel quite *enferma* to see her gazing at you with those cow eyes.' Dolores quite often lapsed into Spanish when she became emotionally overwrought.

He had tried to explain how important Deborah was to him; how able she was with his finances; composing his letters; dealing tactfully with guests, staff, suppliers. He'd pointed out that she had been his right hand for the past thirty-odd years and that he could not just give her notice in so cavalier a fashion. Dolores had become even more adamant.

'So she has this *vasto* importance to you. You choose. You have *her* or me. I go home to Madrid. I divorce you. You marry this . . . this *nuez de nogal* and maybe she make the love besta than me.'

Despite the seriousness of this contretemps, Keven had almost smiled at Dolores' description of the poor unfortunate Deborah. He could not begin to imagine himself making 'the love', as Dolores put it, to a walnut! But there was no arguing with her. She knew perfectly well that Deborah had never, ever been the slightest threat to her marriage. To be rid of her was only a means of gaining a larger control of his life herself.

But he still wanted her. Even at times when she was being most disparaging, critical, cruel, he still desired her exciting, voluptuous body. And even in the impossible eventuality that he did let her leave him, he could no longer afford to do so. Although she was a Roman Catholic and could not divorce him in Spain, she could divorce him in England and he'd be required to give her half his capital – half the huge amount of money the Leisure Times Conglomerate was paying for the Cheyne Manor estate. He'd be left with barely enough to buy a rundown seedy boarding house and he was far too old and tired to do that and work his way up to the top of the pile again. Besides, he wanted Dolores . . .

'I do wish things could have worked out differently, Deborah,' he said, holding out his arms so that he could take her hands in his. Deborah disregarded them. She felt faint and then sick as she tried to come to terms with the fact that her whole life was over. What could she do alone in a bedsit in Ferrybridge? She could not bear the thought of him going to live in Brighton where she might at any time run into him, or, worse, Dolores, in the street or shops. What could she do with herself all day? All evening? Join an old people's club? Do charity work? Take up a hobby? Even with the good reference Mr Harris would undoubtedly give her, at her advanced age she would never get another job as a PA. Perhaps as a secretary, had she mastered the intricacies of the new computer that he'd had installed last year. As it was she could barely cope with the basics. Young people today – even typists – could understand the wretched machine better than she could. Besides, she did not *want* to work for anyone else.

'So I'm to leave, Mr Harris. Would you be so good as to tell me when?'

Kevin looked flustered.

'Not until after St David's Day – that's to say after the handover date. I told Mr O'Donnell – he's the new owner – that it would be a good idea for him to keep you on for a few weeks until the new staff know the ropes. He thought it might be necessary . . . he was talking about getting the decorators in . . .'

Deborah had stopped listening. The first shock had now worn off and the despair she had felt when she realized how she was being tossed to one side like an unwanted plastic bag had given way to a far more bearable emotion. She was trembling with anger . . . anger at Dolores, at fate, at her own stupidity in thinking herself indispensable to Kevin – and most of all anger towards him. She had loved, nurtured and cared for him as that tart of a wife of his had never done. She had loved him entirely unselfishly, asking nothing but his approval of her in return. For thirty-two long years, many of them without even a week's holiday because he said he couldn't manage without her, her first waking thought had been what she might do that day to ease his path. For him to discard her at this time of her life was cruel. If he had at least put up a fight to keep her with him – but she knew without being told that he had submitted without argument to his wife's demands. He should have fought for her as she would have fought for him – had always fought for him. Her love for him had been steadfast, unconditional, constant and totally unselfish. How could he bring himself to cast it aside! It was the most galling way any man could behave.

She looked up and studied him as he sat slumped in his chair. Had she not been so mortified, she might even have felt sorry for him. As a rule, if there were something unpleasant to be said to one of the staff, a guest, a visitor, he would always get her to do the dirty work. Well now he had had to do it himself – repay her years of devotion with not even a month's notice. Three weeks! That was barely time enough to find a place to live. He must have known he was selling up weeks, months ago and had been too cowardly to tell her; afraid, perhaps, that she'd walk out and leave him in the lurch, which she would never ever have done. He ought to have known her better than that. But it wasn't the tardiness of his announcement that tormented her. In a way, she could understand his reluctance to make it. It wasn't that he'd gone about selling the Cheyne Manor estate without a single word to her, hiding the truth from her, hiding letters, documents, taking phone calls on his mobile when he was away from her. It was clear that from the start he had never meant to keep her with him. He'd lied to her, cheated her and was now about to abandon her.

'Debbie, we can still be friends, can't we?'

She looked at him as if he were out of his mind.

'We have never been friends, Mr Harris!' she said. 'I am one of your employees and, as such, I have always done my best to justify my salary. I quite understand that you and Mrs Harris feel it is time to replace me with a younger woman.' She gave a mirthless little laugh. 'It is quite *de rigueur* these days, is it not, for wives to replace their husbands with a younger man, and, if I'm not mistaken, for businessmen such as yourself to replace their elderly secretaries with younger, prettier girls?'

She had of course been speaking sarcastically but Kevin's discomfiture was such that it passed over him and he said with relief: 'I knew you'd understand, Debbie.' He leaned forward to say in a confidential whisper: 'My wife thought you'd probably sue me for unfair dismissal! She said she would open a bottle of champagne tonight if I can tell her that you won't do any such thing.'

So they were to celebrate her departure as if she was no more than a lowly kitchen maid, she thought. Perhaps that was all she had ever really meant to Kevin Harris – someone he could use and discard like an worn-out garment. 'You won't do any such thing,' he'd just said with no regard whatever for the terrible hurt he had inflicted on her.

'No!' she said as she stood up and turned towards the door. 'I won't do any such thing, Mr Harris!'

Nor would she, because she had thought of a far better way to prevent Kevin and his wife from celebrating what amounted to the end of happiness in her life.

*   *   *

Inspector Govern sat at the table in the interview room with DS Beck standing behind him. Across the table from him sat the hotel's assistant manageress, who had just given her name as Deborah Alice Cahill.

'You do understand this statement you wish to make is being recorded, Miss Cahill?' he reminded her. She nodded her head, the scant, thinning grey hair, fastened away from her face by two kirby grips, moving only slightly against her skull. She had refused the cup of tea Sergeant Beck had offered her when she arrived at Ferrybridge Police Station saying she wished to make a statement about the hit-and-run that had taken place last April. It was a formal statement, she insisted – one that could not be invalidated. She had insisted, also, that it was Inspector Govern himself to whom she wished to speak and not the duty police sergeant.

'What exactly is it you wish to tell me, Miss Cahill?' Govern prompted as she remained silent, only her mouth working as if she was swallowing saliva and her false teeth were preventing her from doing so. 'You have some information for me about Mr Rivers' accident on Manor Drive?' he prompted. 'DS Beck has just reminded me that you were the lady who actually found the gentleman on the side of the road.'

'Yes!' Deborah said, her voice quite calm now. 'I did find him, but not on the road as I said in my statement, which I think your sergeant is holding in his hands at the moment, are you not, Sergeant?'

He nodded, handing it to Govern, who flicked through it briefly.

'So where was Mr Rivers, Miss Cahill?'

'He was lying in the rhododendron shrubs at the bottom of the hotel garden. Rusty, my dog, found him, actually. I would never have seen him lying there just inside the boundary wall to the golf course but for my dog. There is a map in the hotel where I can pinpoint the exact spot for you. The 5th fairway runs very close to the wall just there.'

Both Govern and Beck hid their astonishment as they listened to her quiet, reasoned tones.

'So you moved him, Miss Cahill? Can I ask why? I believe it was raining that evening, was it not?'

'Oh, it wasn't because of the rain, Inspector. As soon as I saw Mr Rivers, I knew he was dead – I did a first-aid course many years ago so I knew how to feel his pulse. That's why I left him there and went back to the hotel to inform Mr Harris.'

She paused briefly before adding: 'I must tell the truth and admit to the fact that it was my idea, not Mr Harris's to move the body. You see, I was conscious of the fact that the publicity would be very disadvantageous to the hotel if the press got hold of the fact that a dead man had been found in the hotel gardens. It was not a place where Mr Rivers might have gone where he could suddenly have died from a heart attack. I realized that it had to be either suicide or murder, and, of the two, murder seemed more probable. Had it been suicide, he could have gassed himself in his car or taken an overdose, or jumped off the pier in preference to hiding in a remote shrubbery.'

'Very perceptive of you, Miss Cahill!' Govern said caustically. 'You do realize, don't you, that moving a body is an offence? I would like to remind you of the caution DS Beck read to you whilst you were waiting for me to arrive.'

Deborah returned his gaze with a slight lift of her eyebrows.

'I'm not exactly ignorant of the law, Inspector. I do know what I'm doing, I assure you.'

She proceeded to relate how she and Kevin Harris had waited a while before carrying Mr Rivers' body to the hotel garage, putting him in the hotel estate car and only then driving him to the hospital. As she had anticipated, she now told the inspector, Mr Harris's and her own statements at that time saying that they had found Mr Rivers on the side of Manor Road made his death appear to be a hit-and-run accident rather than a murder. Their actions, she added, had fulfilled her intention, which was to avoid unwelcome publicity. Such as there was in the local newspapers soon wound down, and that, she concluded, had been the end of the matter.

Govern shook his head.

'Not quite, Miss Cahill. After Mrs Russell's murder, I looked more deeply into Mr Rivers' death. I suspected that we had a murder rather than an accident on our hands. The difficulty, of course, lay in discovering who committed it and why! You realize, don't you, that the information you have just given me would have been of great help to us had you told the truth at the time. I shall have to take both you and Mr Harris into custody and, in due course, you will be charged with attempting to pervert the course of justice. However, as you have seen fit to confess your offence the court may take this into consideration.'

Deborah nodded, her expression impassive. It was only when Govern asked her what had motivated her to make this confession at this late stage that her face took on an entirely different expression – one Govern found hard to interpret until she spoke.

'Mr Harris has sold the hotel and will be removing to Brighton,' she said. 'It seemed to me that since we were both leaving the locality, one of us ought to speak out in order that the murderer, if such there was, should be brought to justice.'

'So you planned to remove with Mr and Mrs Harris to Brighton?' Govern asked. 'I'm afraid the legal position you are now both in may make this impossible until after your case has been heard. Doubtless the sale of the hotel will go through if it has not already done so, but your plans to start a new venture will be disrupted.'

To his astonishment, Deborah's face broke into a wide smile.

'Not *my* plans,' she said. 'I am not to go with them. After thirty-two years of service, and only three weeks' notice, I have been made redundant, so I shall be remaining in Ferrybridge if I am not to be incarcerated in one of Her Majesty's prisons!'

'My God!' David Beck said as the duty sergeant took Deborah away. 'Are you thinking what I'm thinking, sir?'

Govern nodded.

'Without doubt – hell hath no fury like a woman scorned!'

'Puts a new light on the Rivers case!' Beck said. 'Looks like you were right, sir, and it was murder.'

'Yes, but by whom?' Govern said thoughtfully. 'Soon as the sergeant has finished with our Miss Cahill, we're going up to the hotel, David. I want to see exactly where the old girl found Rivers' body!'

Much later, Rose and Poppy were to speculate on the remarkable twist of fate that there had been no tutorials on the day of Miss Cahill's confession. They were taking advantage of a moderately warm and sunny February day to play tennis when they saw the police inspector and his assistant with Kevin and Deborah between them, walking slowly down to the shrubbery. They stared at one another with identical expressions of anxiety. Pretending to be picking up loose tennis balls, they watched as Deborah halted and pointed to the shrubbery where they had tipped Gordon Rivers' body. They saw the inspector bend down and look beneath the rhododendron bushes. A moment later, Beck was staring over the boundary wall on to the golf course. There was an exchange of words and then the sergeant produced a roll of white tape and proceeded to encircle the area.

'Oh no!' Poppy whispered.

'Surely it *can't* have been Miss Cahill and Mr Harris who moved him!' Rose murmured.

But they were left in no further doubt when, as the foursome passed the tennis court on their way back to the hotel, they could see the handcuffs on the couple's wrists.

Fifteen

Jason né Arnold Bellman, had not wasted his time in prison. Owing to the nature of his offence, and most prisoners' antipathy towards any man who molested children, he'd had very few friends. One of those few was a Canadian safe-breaker who had killed the man who'd grassed on him. By the time Jason was released, although far from being a safe-breaker, he was capable of making duplicate keys for moderately simple locks. Since coming to England he had not made use of this skill, determined as he was to keep his new identity from any close inspection.

Now, as he drove into the golf club car park, he noticed that the door of the greenkeeper's hut was ajar. It crossed his mind that this was a bit casual; anyone at any time could nip in and pinch one of the implements Joe kept in it; not one of the mowers, of course, but a strimmer, hedge clippers, rakes . . . He was about to include weed-killer as something a person might want to steal for their garden use when he checked himself. Weed-killer would almost certainly be locked up in the metal cabinet in the greenkeeper's hut, which he kept especially for such things . . . weed-killer and maybe that stuff Bob Heath had been talking about last month which gassed moles?

Jason remained seated in his car, his mind working furiously as he tried to recall his time in the product development department of the asphalt company where he'd been employed prior to his imprisonment. There'd been one job where his knowledge of chemistry had proved particularly useful. If he could get a glimpse of the list of chemicals on the canister

155

containing the pellets used in mole killing, he could ascertain whether there was anything strong enough to kill a man.

Jason's breathing quickened as his mind, too, started racing. For weeks now he'd been trying to think of a way of despatching his blackmailer once and for all but without any hint of danger to himself. People said there was no such thing as a perfect murder but he didn't agree. Perfect murders, he told himself, may well be numerous but not listed, as they were never discovered! People disappeared without trace. People were killed and their murderers never detected. All that was needed was a cool brain; time taken to work out a safe way to execute a killing, and establish an alibi. In his case, he could gamble on the fact that Barry Russell had told no one of his activities, so although everyone who knew Barry would initially be suspect, his motive would be unknown.

Staring for some time through his windscreen, he saw no sign of Joe. He glanced at his watch. One thirty. Perhaps Joe had gone for his lunch – a perk of the job allowing him to enjoy the same food as the golfers but eaten in the back kitchen. Nor was there anyone else in the car park. Opening his car door, Jason slipped quickly across the parking space and into Joe's shed. Almost immediately he caught sight of a metal cabinet up against the wall behind the sit-on lawn mower. With a quick look outside to make sure Joe was not on his way back, he leaned across the mower and tried the cabinet door. As he thought, it was locked; but typical of most honest unsuspecting members of the human race, Joe had hung the key on a nail on a heavy timber strut to the side of the steel cupboard.

Jason wasted no more time and was on his way out of the hut when Joe came walking towards him from the kitchen.

'I was looking for you, Joe!' he lied easily. 'I wanted to congratulate you on the state of the greens. They're running really true.'

'Thank you, sir! I reckon that day or two of sunshine helped to dry them out a bit. Sorry you had to wait. I'd gone for my lunch. One to two o'clock I always have it.'

'I should have remembered,' Jason said, gloating inwardly now he knew he could come any day with a bar of soap in his pocket and take an impression of the key.

A week later, Jason not only knew that, used correctly, the pellets employed to gas the moles would be lethal to a man, but he had half a cannister of them, securely contained in a tobacco tin. Now all that was needed for him to despatch Barry Russell was the less easy task of finding somewhere to do the deed. A further week passed whilst Jason sat at his blank computer screen night after night trying to work out where he might carry out the murder whilst remaining one hundred per cent safe from even the tiniest hint of suspicion. The solution came to him at the weekend when he was playing golf with Bob Heath. Bob was regaling him with one of his usual not-very-funny jokes.

It was about a golfer who confessed to a priest that he had used the f-word when he'd missed a hole-in-one when his ball hit the pin and ricocheted off it, stopping an inch or two away. 'Is that when you used the f-word?' the priest asked. 'No!' said the golfer. 'It was when I missed the f . . . ing putt.'

He waited for Jason's laugh, which was not forthcoming. Jason had been about to lob his ball on to the green of the 3rd hole when he saw Barry Russell emerging on to the fairway from the bushes fronting his back garden.

'Lucky so-and-so!' Bob said, forgetting his joke. 'Wish I had my own buggy. Must be handy coming down your garden path, opening the shed and driving the thing straight on to the course.'

Jason mishit his ball with his wedge and heard Bob chuckle.

'Reckon that's lost you the hole,' he said as he putted his own ball to within three feet of the flag.

Jason put his club back in his golf bag and said casually: 'Do you mean Barry actually has a shed for his buggy at the bottom of his garden?'

Bob nodded.

'He used to keep it at the club when he and Betty bought

157

it a year or two ago – second hand, of course. Then she had the shed built for it last Christmas; and she bought him some clubs, too. Some people have all the luck!' he added, sighing, as they moved up on to the green where Jason's ball had landed at least fifteen yards from the flag. 'Barry's one of them lucky ones,' Bob continued. 'He came into a small legacy a few months ago – or so he told Melville when he remarked that he seemed unusually flush. Believe it or not, Barry was standing drinks all round at the bar, and you know what a skinflint he usually is.'

Jason's whole being was flooded suddenly with anger. Barry Russell's so-called legacy consisted of *his* payments, which he estimated to be over two thousand pounds. He followed Bob across the path leading to the fourth tee, his mind working furiously. If he hadn't already made up his mind to put an end to the blackmail, he'd be doing so now, he told himself. Unwittingly, Bob had just pointed out how it could be done. All he had to do was get Barry to agree to him using the buggy shed as a dropping zone for his cash.

It shouldn't be too difficult to convince Barry, he told himself as he lined up his putt. For one thing, he'd point out that the wastebin outside the greenkeeper's shed was far too public to be the ideal dropping and collecting point. For another, how simple it would be for him to put the money in Barry's buggy shed when he played one of his regular nine-hole practice rounds. If, when playing on his own, he was seen stopping on the 3rd fairway and slipping into the bushes opposite Barry's back gate, he had only to say he'd sliced his ball and was looking for it. Any golfers following him would expect him to obey the rules and stand back and wave them through.

Barry, he now reckoned, should be delighted with the plan since at any time he had only to walk down his garden path and collect his money, or, if he preferred, pick it up when he parked his buggy back in its shed after a game. As for himself, once he had established what time of day Barry usually returned home following his weekly men's foursome, he could conceal himself near the buggy shed and wait for him to unlock the door. Or, better still, he could make a duplicate key, and if it was raining or uncomfortably cold he could let himself into the shed to wait for the sound of Barry opening his garden gate.

Barry was without suspicion when, three weeks later, Jason outlined his suggestion for a change of 'dropping zone'. He could see the danger of leaving the money in the wastebin in so public a place – a danger if not for Jason then for himself. Anyone seing him poking about amongst the empty beer cans and plastic wrappers would wonder what on earth he was doing. He even thanked Jason for thinking up this new venue for them both. To Jason's ironical amusement, Barry even told him how he put the key to the buggy shed under a brick behind the water butt so that Jason could leave the money safely locked up inside.

Barry was now of the firm opinion that Jason was if not exactly gay, certainly a weak, soft-centred chap afraid of his own shadow. He had recently upped the amount he was demanding for his silence and the man had paid up without a murmur. The fellow obviously had a regular income over and above his job, he concluded, and since Betty's capital had not been forthcoming, Jason's cash would continue to do very well instead.

The sky was overcast and it had just started to drizzle when a week later Jason decided he had no need to delay carrying out his plan any longer. With his usual precision, he had read the label on the canister containing the aluminium phosphide pellets and knew exactly what was needed and how he must proceed. He'd checked the pro's list of tee-off times for the day's play and seen that Barry's foursome was going out at eleven o'clock. With the weather threatening rain the course should not be crowded, so they might expect an easy four-hour round. That would mean Barry getting back to the club-house by four at the latest; he'd have time for a quick drink and be on his way home around five. By then it would be almost dark. If he, Jason, could tee off on the first around three o'clock, telling anyone who was still about that he intended doing the 1st, 2nd, 3rd and 9th holes for a quick practice, he'd be nicely outside Barry's back garden around three thirty – in perfect time to unlock the buggy shed, check that there was water in the watering can and shelter inside if it was raining and wait for Barry to arrive.

Jason just managed to sink his putt on the 1st green when the first heavy raindrops began to spatter down on his head and shoulders. He looked back towards the clubhouse and saw, not surprisingly, that no one was following him. He decided not to bother to drive off the 2nd but to hurry along the rough in the shelter of the wooded perimeter of the course. No need to pretend to an onlooker that he was looking for his ball! Despite his now dripping jacket and trousers, Jason grinned as he went through the gate and, dropping his golf bag behind the water butt, he put his index finger and thumb into his left-handed golf glove to avoid leaving fingerprints, and picked up the key to the shed from under the brick.

Now familiar with the interior, he glanced at the rusty watering can in the corner, and as he needed water for his gas pellets to be effective he wasted no time in filling it up. There was no window, since the small concrete building had been intended for the buggy only, so he had no need to seal up any ventilators. On a previous visit he had ascertained that the up-and-over door fitted snugly on all sides, thus ensuring that the concrete structure was almost completely air proof.

In the distance a dog barked, and through the ornamental laburnum trees, now bare of leaves, a light came on in the window of one of the neighbours' houses. On the far side of the garden the windows of the other neighbouring house were dark – probably commuters or people who worked in Ferrybridge and would not be home for another hour or two, Jason decided. Despite the cold wind now blowing in through the open entrance to the shed, Jason was sweating profusely. Every nerve in his body seemed to be alive, tingling with anticipation. He had never killed a man before. In prison there'd been several lifers who'd bragged about the kick it had given them to take a life. In nearly every case it had been an act of revenge – a man whose wife had cheated on him and run off with his kids; another whose neighbour had maliciously cut down the yew hedge he'd been nurturing all his adult life. In both cases there had been provocation, and each man maintained that, despite the consequences, revenge had indeed been sweet.

Only now did Jason fully understand that emotion. Barry was like a parasite, slowly sucking him dry, preying on his fears, his demands ever increasing. Men like him needed to be wiped off the face of the earth just as the two lifers had maintained. Some thought *he* should be snuffed out because of his crimes, but he had never intentionally *hurt* a child; he loved children; and after the savage beatings he himself had received as a boy from his father whilst his mother had watched unmoving he could never love an adult human being. Children were there to be loved and . . .

His thoughts reverted sharply to the present. He went out of the shed and, locking it, put the key in its hiding place and disappeared round the back to wait. He had time now to make a last check that he'd taken every possible precaution against detection; that he'd left no tiny detail uncovered – even to wearing the size nine Dunlop golf shoes which exactly matched those he had noted Barry had in his locker at the club to confuse footprints. Mentally he went through the list – a large cotton tea towel to gag him; the ratchet strap he'd bought in Ferrybridge to secure Barry to his buggy seat; water in the can; a surgical mask to protect his own mouth and nose from the fumes; the tin containing the pellets which would give out their lethal poisonous vapour; and finally the suicide note, which he had carefully worded to explain why Barry had chosen to end his life.

It would be the perfect murder, he was congratulating himself at the same moment as he heard the sound of the petrol-engine buggy. It stopped momentarily whilst Barry opened his garden gate, then started again as it was driven towards the shed. Pulling his mask down over his face, Jason's heartbeat quickened and he slid round the other side of the shed where he could not be seen. Holding his breath, he waited whilst Barry took his own key from his pocket and opened the shed door. Seconds later there was the sound of a bump as the buggy went over the concrete slip of the floor. As Jason moved quickly forward, Barry shut off the ignition.

It took less than five seconds for Jason to stand behind the buggy and throw the looped ratchet strap over Barry's head, shoulders and upper arms, wrenching it tight. Barry barely had time to shout a few loud words of protest before Jason had secured the tea towel over his mouth, silencing his muffled cries. Despite the man's now frantic struggles, Jason was able to pull the strap even tighter, anchoring him so securely to his seat that Barry's hopelessly inadequate attempts to free himself slowed and then ceased altogether. Only the terrified expression in his eyes revealed his desperate fear.

Jason now pulled the door of the shed halfway down, shutting out most of the evening light but leaving him enough room to make his escape before the poisonous fumes overcame him as well as his victim. With a last look at the man he was about to kill, Jason tossed the typed suicide note into the back of the buggy and, turning quickly, emptied the pellets out of the tin into the watering can. This done he raced outside, pulled the door of the shed closed, and, still wearing his glove, he turned the key in the lock.

For a few moments, Jason stood perfectly still in the darkness. He could hear the steady dripping of raindrops on the carpet of leaves beneath the trees. An owl hooted and away in the far distance came the wailing siren of an ambulance. Was it safe yet to move? It might be several hours before he could be certain Barry was dead, the fumes from the pellets slowly poisoning his lungs as, presumably, it killed the unfortunate moles, he told himself. Did he dare leave him? Return later to remove the gag and strap? There was absolutely no way on earth Barry could escape from the shed. Unless . . . only now did it occur to Jason that if somehow, by some miracle, Russell managed to struggle free, he might start up the engine of the buggy and back it as fast as he could against the locked door. If it didn't give way at the first attempt it might well do so by the second or third.

This, he told himself firmly, was the distorted thinking of a frightened man. He had nothing whatever to be frightened about. Joe, for one, had not even noticed the missing pellets. No one had seen him leave the golf course and he had only to take the greatest care as he returned to the clubhouse.

Jason smiled as he recalled that many years ago a man had committed suicide in Canada by inhaling poison gas used to kill moles. He might even mention it in a throwaway line if at some future date doubts were expressed in the club about Barry's choice of such a bizarre method of killing oneself.

Relaxing now, Jason took off his glove and, tucking it in his back pocket, he collected his golf bag from behind the shed and glanced at his watch. Barry had returned home later than he had expected, and he saw that it was now close on six o'clock. With at least a twenty minutes' walk ahead of him back to the clubhouse, he decided he might attract less attention if he retraced his steps to the 1st tee and went straight into the car park without going near the clubhouse.

He listened one last time to ensure there was no noise coming from within the shed or movements from either of the adjoining properties or from the golf course. It was time to go. He shouldered his bag of clubs and felt his way in what was now total darkness between the trees out on to the golf course. Once again, he congratulated himself as he reached his car without encountering a soul.

Back in his cottage, Jason poured himself a large whisky, lit the fire in the sitting-room grate, which he'd laid before he went out that morning, and sat down heavily in his armchair. Despite the fact that he knew he had safely accomplished his plan without detection, his hands holding the glass were trembling and he could feel his heart thumping in his chest. Nervous reaction, he told himself. Not surprising seeing that this was the first time he'd killed a man. All he had left to do now to complete his plan was to return to the shed around midnight when no one would be around to see him, and remove the gag and strap – tasks that would take him no more than a few minutes.

He looked at the watch strapped round his left wrist and his heart jolted. Where was the golf glove he'd used at the shed? He'd put it as he always did in the back pocket of his trousers when he locked the buggy shed. With a rising sense of panic, Jason now recalled that it wasn't there when he'd changed into dry clothes before coming downstairs to light the fire.

His heart now thudding furiously, Jason raced back upstairs, desperate to find that the glove had fallen from his trousers; or even that he had put it absentmindedly in the pocket of his anorak. A cold sweat now pervaded his body as with desperation he went out to the car to check his golf bag, the floor of the boot, even, ridiculous though it was, under the car seats.

Trembling now with an icy fear, Jason returned to his sitting room and poured himself a second whisky. He still had one hope – that the glove may have dropped on to the fairway on his way back to the car park; it might even be on the ground where his car was parked, he told himself, Nevertheless, he was deeply afraid that this vital piece of evidence was now lying somewhere outside Barry's buggy shed. Could he be certain of finding it now that it was pitch dark?

For fifteen minutes Jason sat staring into the fire as he faced the danger he might be in if he couldn't retrieve it, and tried to decide what to do. He could drive back to the clubhouse, check the parking lot, the fairway, but if anyone saw him they would think he was crazy to do such a thing in the dark and rain. Like it or not, if he was to rid himself of his present unnerving anxiety, he would have to search in Barry's garden first, and if his glove was not there he could feel fairly certain that it was on one of the fairways or in the car park. As it was, he'd planned to go to the buggy shed at midnight to remove the gag and strap, but now his growing fear that he had indeed dropped his glove by the shed overrode his decision to leave the visit so late.

The rain was now falling steadily and it was inconceivable, he told himself, that either of Barry's neighbours would be in their gardens in the dark and wet. He would wait until ten o'clock – that should be late enough to be sure he'd be unobserved. He would take his small pencil torch, keep the beam close to the ground and hopefully find his glove before he entered the buggy shed. Apart from believing this was the best decision, he was dreading the moment when he would have to confront the sight of the man he had killed. He harboured a totally irrational fear that Russell might not be fully dead – and this despite knowing full well that the poisonous fumes would have killed him in a matter of minutes.

He stood up and paced the floor, his mind working furiously. He would go to the back drive of the hotel where it joined Beechwood Avenue. The drive was used only by tradesmen and couples having sex in the backs of their cars at night, so he knew he could leave his car there unnoticed for the twenty minutes or so it would take him to skirt the wooded boundary at the end of the Beechwood Avenue back gardens, nip into The Gables by the back gate, check the garden path, shed and its surrounds. He calculated that the chances of him being seen on a dark, rainy winter night were minimal.

He had nothing to worry about, he reckoned as he poured himself a third drink, unless he failed to find his glove. Once again, Jason's heart started hammering. His forehead and the palms of his hands were wet with sweat. After half an hour had passed, he decided that the waiting was proving intolerable. He would leave in an hour's time, when all the back gardens would surely be deserted.

At last the hour hand had moved to ten o'clock and he drove to Cheyne Manor estate, parked his car in the back drive and made his way on foot towards Barry's back gate. Rain clouds obscured any moonlight there might have been and he was obliged to use his pencil torch to avoid branches and rabbit holes. As he went quietly through the half-open gate, he could see no lights shining from Russell's house or from that of his neighbours.

But as he was searching desperately around in the under-growth, the back door in one of the neighbours' houses opened, and a man's voice said: 'Out you go, Rex. I'm not walking you this time of night!'

Jason paused, holding his breath as the man spoke a second time.

'Get on out there when I tell you. Go on! Shoo!'

Jason could now hear a dog whining before the man spoke again, this time with considerable exasperation.

'For God's sake, Rex, a bit of rain won't hurt you. Now get out or I'll kick you out!'

Jason's instinct was to slip away as quickly as possible, but he resisted the urge, telling himself that if the dog so obvi-ously hated the rain, it would not stay out longer than was necessary to lift its leg. He waited motionless until at last he heard the man's voice calling the dog inside. But, quiet although he had been, the animal must have heard him. The neighbour was now swearing at it and threatening dire consequences if he had to come out and get it.

Jason's heart thudded in his chest as he heard the dog, now within a few yards of him, rustling excitedly in the hedge dividing the two gardens. Realizing that the animal had scented him, Jason now decided to gamble on the glove being else-where and to abandon his search rather than to risk being found on the premises. He could go back to his car, wait an hour or so and return later to see to the dead man and make a final search for his glove. Meanwhile, the quicker he was out of the garden the better.

In his haste to get away, but not daring to use his torch, Jason tripped over a garden rake which had been propped against the side of the shed. The noise of his fall alerted the dog to his exact whereabouts and, ignoring its owner's shouts, it stood barking furiously as it attempted to get through the hedge. Jason struggled frantically to his feet. He heard a woman's voice demanding to know what was going on and the man replying that he was about to go and investigate.

As quickly as he could, Jason stumbled through the darkness back on to the golf course. His heart thumping furiously in his chest, he was unaware of the brambles scratching his face or even the sharp pain as he twisted his ankle on a tree root. He was also unaware that the glove he had been searching for so desperately was lying on the ground by the side of Barry Russell's garden gate.

Sixteen

February

'So it is murder, not suicide, sir,' Sergeant Beck said as he and Govern watched the ambulance take Barry's stretchered body away to the mortuary. On either side of them, the neighbours in dressing gowns stood in their doorways, wide eyed with curiosity, watching the proceedings. It was the dog, Rex, who was the hero of the event, barking so interminably as it tried to get through the hedge into Barry's garden that, ignoring the darkness and the rain, the owner had gone to investigate. Despite the continued noise his dog was making, Barry's neighbour had seen no sign of an intruder. The terrier was scratching at the shed door, which, the man ascertained, was safely locked. After a moment's hesitation, he'd decided to go up the path to Barry's back door and alert him to the fact that there might be burglars around. There were no lights on in the house and, after peering into the windows and seeing no sign of life, he'd checked that Barry's car was in the garage.

Both men belonged to the Neighbourhood Watch scheme and over the years had kept an eye on each other's properties. He'd sensed that something was amiss. For one thing, Barry never went anywhere on foot; he even took his car down to the nearby Ferrydene post office-cum-village store. After a brief consultation with his wife, who had agreed at once that he could not leave matters as they were, he'd dialled 999.

Govern took a last look round the shed. The buggy had been removed in order to make room for the stretcher-bearers

168

and it was now empty except for a battery charger in one corner and the watering can in the other. Nevertheless, the fumes from the gas still lingered faintly in the atmosphere,

'Intended to look like a suicide,' Govern replied to his sergeant's comment. 'Might even have got away with it if the neighbour hadn't decided there was something fishy going on. So the murderer didn't have time to get back into the shed and remove the strap and gag before he scarpered.'

He broke off, concentrating once more on the piece of paper he was holding.

'". . . *missing Betty so much, I can't go on . . .*"' he read aloud. 'No, I don't think for one moment he wrote this. Remember how positive we were he'd actively hated his wife?'

Beck grinned.

'Yes, sir, and she wasn't that fond of him, was she? Anyway, she's well and truly off the list of possible murderers.'

It was several minutes before Govern spoke again. Beck was accustomed to these prolonged silences. They usually meant his boss was having one of his intuitions but was seeking a way to prove his theory. He looked at his watch. It was now two thirty a.m. and they'd both been up at seven.

Tired though he was, he was not in the least surprised when Govern said suddenly: 'Right! Get this shed locked and we're going up to the house. I want to give it a thorough going-over before the foot brigade arrive. Can't say I regret this particular chap's death but I do intend to get the man who killed him.'

Two policemen had cordoned off the premises of The Gables and another stood by the front door barring entry. Govern showed no sign of fatigue as he and Beck went into the house. He was like a pointer who scented game, his nerve ends tingling with a certainty that somehow Barry Russell's death was tied up with his wife's murder, and possibly with Gordon Rivers' murder – none of which made sense. There was always a motive for murder, and whilst Russell might have murdered his wife hoping to inherit her money, he must have known he'd be instantly suspect. Nor had their relationship been one where the man had killed his wife in a jealous passion! Nor, finally, had he, Govern, been able to establish that Russell had killed her.

As for Gordon Rivers – the Cahill woman's extraordinary confession had led them to suspect that he was probably murdered by a hotel resident; but none of the residents at the time proved to have the slightest reason for bumping him off – indeed, other than the two old ladies and the twins, only two or three others even knew the man. As soon as they had dealt with this new murder, they'd have to reopen the Rivers case.

He was coming ever more steadily to the conclusion that the murders were linked. But he'd deal with this one first.

'We'll get the fingerprint chaps up tomorrow morning,' he said now to Beck. 'For what's left of tonight, I intend to go through Russell's house with . . .'

'. . . a nit comb?' Beck finished.

Govern frowned but his voice held a hint of humour as he reproached his assistant.

'For God's sake, DS Beck, will you please start taking your job a bit more seriously. Now open the door and start looking!'

Not that he had, as yet, any reason to look for anything in particular, Govern told himself. He was motivated by nothing more than a hunch, but in the past his hunches had paid off, as had happened in the Millers Lane murders, and it was for that reason that he had insisted the DCI allow him to be notified of any untoward event that took place at Cheyne Manor Hotel or the golf club and handle the situation himself.

Despite his hunch that he himself was on the verge of unravelling the Cheyne estate murders, it was Sergeant Beck who inadvertently found the first important lead.

'Look at this, sir!' he said as he emerged from the late Betty Russell's bedroom. He was holding an album of wedding photographs, one of which had half slipped out of its holder. It portrayed Betty and Barry Russell outside a church, Betty looking young, pretty, radiant; Barry looking surly, as if bored by the proceedings.

'There's the radiant bride but hardly the ardent groom!' Beck said. 'Maybe you're right, sir, and he bumped her off from sheer boredom. If the marriage started like that, what must it have been like thirty years later?'

But Govern wasn't looking at the wedding photograph. He had seen the corner of a piece of writing paper, which he now eased away from behind the picture. As Govern gave a tiny gasp, Beck looked curiously over his shoulder. It was a letter written on headed notepaper in a large, round, feminine hand.

Dear Inspector Govern, *it read*,

It is now four weeks since I overheard the facts about Mr Gordon Rivers' murder. Barry, my husband, thinks I would be stupid to report these facts to you as you will almost certainly disbelieve them. He told me to forget what I had heard but although I have tried to do so I cannot forget about it, and it is preventing me sleeping at night.

The letter then went on to relate the conversation between the Matheson twins which she had overheard in the ladies' changing room.

I know you may think this too incredible to take seriously, *she continued*, but you have only to see how nervy and dispirited those girls are these days to know that something in their lives has gone very wrong. I would be very grateful, if you do decide to act on this information, that you don't disclose how you discovered the facts as my husband would be very angry with me. I know he is only trying to prevent me making a fool of myself, but he seems to be taking this very personally and has said he won't ever forgive me if I tell you what I heard. It is a chance I now have to take as my conscience will not allow me to remain silent any longer.

Govern drew a long breath and exhaled slowly before saying: 'There's the answer to Rivers' murder. If my memory serves me right, one or other or both of those girls left the golf club party early that night – took the short cut back to the hotel. If one of them killed Rivers, as Mrs Russell relates, it explains how Miss Cahill's dog came to find his body where it was dumped.'

Sergeant Beck nodded excitedly.

'And if Mr Russell was so adamant that his missus didn't speak out, he must have had a reason, which could have been . . .'

'Blackmail!' said Govern, who was a jump ahead of him. 'Mrs Russell writes this letter to me, is persuaded once again not to send it just yet; husband realizes his blackmailing activities are on the verge of discovery and . . .'

'Bumps her off. But how? You'd think someone would have seen him doing the dirty deed in the middle of the 5th fairway. Damn dangerous thing to risk.'

'You forget he had that buggy. What price killing her before he left home and then whisking her over to the 5th and tipping her into the bunker? Clever way to make us think that her murderer was more likely to have nipped across the fairway from the footpath – which we did think.'

Govern remained silent for a moment as he walked over to the uncurtained window and stared out into the darkness. Dawn was still a long way off but he was too full of adrenalin to feel tired. He turned suddenly to his waiting sergeant.

'See if there is anything else relevant you can find,' he said. 'A paying-in bank book, a bank statement – something of that sort.'

Sergeant Beck disappeared for five minutes and then came back beaming.

'Just look at this, sir – meticulous accounts of the man's blackmailing activities.'

'Accounts in the plural?' Govern asked, quick to notice the plural.

'Yes, sir. Look at this!'

It was a small, black, year 2004 golf diary measuring about eighteen by ten centimetres. It contained the usual dates of club activities, tournaments, invitation games, committee meetings followed by a straightforward day-by-day diary for the owner to fill in. Turning to the month of April, among Russell's personal golf dates, was the announcement of Gordon Rivers' murder. Further on came the listing Govern was looking for: R&P, £100.

There followed other entries of £150 going up to £200, until a total of £900 was listed and the comment: *Not bad, but R&P now skint. Resume demands Xmas.*

'So that's that!' Sergeant Beck said with a sigh of satisfaction.

'Not necessarily!' Govern argued as he turned over page after page until he found what he wanted. 'See here, David? Once blackmailers get a taste for easy money, they always want to go on with it. He pointed to an entry for £200. A week later there was a further entry: *J. A. £200.*

'So all we have to do now is find out who J. A. is, why he was being blackmailed and if he has a perfect alibi for last night, because it's a ninety per cent cert that Russell's killer is the mystery J. A.'

It was a minute or two before Sergeant Beck spoke, then it was in an unusually quiet voice.

'There's a chap up at the club I played golf with a while ago. I rather liked him but you warned me not to get too close. Odd sort of fellow, born in this country but spent most of his life in Canada. Engineer, I think he said he was.'

'David, will you stop meandering and tell me who the hell you're talking about?'

'Yes, sir, it's Jason Armitage, though God knows why anyone should be blackmailing him.'

'First light, go check his alibi,' Govern said. 'We've done more than enough tonight. Time we got a bit of sleep, because there'll be a great deal to do tomorrow. If this J. A. fellow did kill Russell, then we know why, but we've got to find evidence to prove it. He won't have been so daft as to leave fingerprints, although we'll have them taken just in case.'

But when morning came there was no need for finger-print experts, or for Jason to provide an alibi. Let out for his early morning run, the terrier, Rex, decided to burrow his way for the second time through the hedge dividing his master's garden from the Russells'. He'd heard all the strange noises coming from next door, seen men in uniform, even an Alsatian on a lead, and wanted to know what was going on. There wasn't much to see. The buggy shed was securely locked with a policeman on guard. Betty's tame robin was hopping agitatedly in the overhanging laburnum tree. But Rex was not relying on sight. He had scented something unusual by the gate leading to the golf course. It was wet, muddy and half covered by leaves. He grabbed it securely in his mouth, shaking it as if it were a dead rat, and leaped the dividing hedge into his own garden. Ignoring the policeman's shout, he ran indoors with his trophy, his tail wagging furiously.

'What you got hold of now, you little devil?' the man asked as he put down his early morning cup of tea. 'More rubbish?'

But it wasn't rubbish. Rex proudly presented his master with Jason Armitage's golf glove.

Inspector Govern was informed of all this as he walked into the police station shortly before eight o'clock. Beck was waiting for him.

'If one of those girls did kill Mr Rivers,' he said, 'which one do you think did it, sir?'

Govern sighed.

'I'm not guessing, David. I'll interview them after I've seen Jason Armitage.'

'If they *are* guilty and you give them a chance to confess,' Beck said, 'it could make their sentence that much lighter when it came to the crunch, couldn't it, sir?'

By mid-morning, knowing that his glove had been found and was even now being tested for DNA, Jason made a full confession, admitting that Barry Russell had been blackmailing

him. Once he was safely under lock and key at Ferrybridge
Police Station, Govern turned his attention once more to the
Matheson twins. He was no longer in any doubt about their
guilt, but he was not looking forward to what must now be
done.

'Get down to the hotel, David, and bring them in for questioning,' he said gruffly.

Remembering how he had fancied the Matheson girls, Beck
was far from happy with his assignment. He was even less
happy about it when he arrived at the hotel to learn from Pepe
that they'd checked out of the hotel at lunch time. Unable to
reach his boss on his mobile, he raced back to the police
station. Govern had returned to his desk when Beck burst into
the room.

'Seems they've left the hotel, sir. I spoke to the concierge
who told me they went off an hour ago with their father.'

'With their father?' Govern echoed. 'But why on earth . . .'

'Pepe said the twins had been trying to get their father on
the telephone for the past two days. Sir Julian rang them first
thing this morning. Seems he was in Paris on business and he
told them they had to return home immediately and he'd come
and collect them. Pepe was quite impressed because he'd
arrived at the hotel around one thirty having – believe it or
not – hired a plane and flown over to Lydd airport. Then he'd
hired a car to get to the hotel.'

Seeing Govern's anxious expression, he added quickly: 'And
that's not all, sir. Pepe gathered from Sir Julian that the rush
was on because of a life-and-death situation with a dying aunt,
but then he asked Pepe to find out times of car ferries. I was
quite impressed with Pepe's IQ when he pointed out that it
was a bit off – Sir Julian's James Bond-style arrival because
of an impending death, and then going back to France on a
car ferry. Why not fly back?'

Govern was now pacing the floor, his eyes on Beck's face.

'Something more?' he prompted.

Beck nodded.

'It seems the twins had one small suitcase each and Pepe

said he had to go down to the cellar to fetch their father's golf clubs. That's all they took. Their father paid the girls' bills plus a very hefty tip for Pepe and they left at two o'clock. One of the twins told him they were going to Dover to catch the boat ferry to Calais.'

Govern now spoke with a quiet urgency.

'Tell Mandy to find out the times of departure of the afternoon ferries ... pronto!' he said. 'With a bit of luck we've still time to catch up with them.'

Beck made a quick telephone call to the DC, and, efficient as always, she returned the call within minutes.

'The afternoon ferries leave at two thirty, three fifteen, four fifteen, five, five forty-five ...'

'Enough!' Govern interrupted. 'Get a car pronto, David!'

A further phone call established they had approximately a two-hour journey ahead of them.

'If Matheson left at two o'clock,' he said to Beck as they hurried down to the car park, 'he'll miss the four-fifteen ferry for sure.' He looked at his watch and calculated: 'He should make the five o'clock. If he misses that, they'll be waiting on the dock for the five forty-five. So step on it, Beck. We need to move fast. If we go like Concorde, we'll catch them.'

They took one of the police cars instead of Govern's BMW so that they could use the flashing blue lights and break all the speed limits. During the journey, Beck was speculating as to why Sir Juliian Matheson chose to travel from Dover to Calais rather than from the much closer port of Newhaven, crossing to Dieppe.

'Possibly Matheson has opted for that route so they can catch a train to Paris and get the overnight car carrier-cum-sleeper to the South of France,' Govern suggested. 'Or maybe he thought we'd suppose him to have selected the nearest port and the girls weren't supposed to mention Dover to the concierge.'

Then he was silent for a while before saying: 'Presumably by now they've got rid of—' He broke off before saying excitedly: 'The golf clubs – the ones their father made Pepe fetch from the cellar; the ones they took with them. Good God, Beck, two and two are beginning to make four. What was the club the pathologist said could have inflicted the blow that killed Rivers?'

'A number one driver, sir. There's virtually no angle on them, you see and . . .' he broke off as Govern swerved momentarily before righting the wheel and then continued. 'She was using her father's driver – the twin called Poppy. Just after Gorden Rivers' death, we asked everyone to produce their drivers, remember, sir? I asked Poppy Matheson about hers because it seemed so long for her. She must have swapped them – put her club in her father's bag where no one would ever think of looking for it and used his.'

'We're guessing, David, but I'd lay a hundred to one we're right.'

As they drew up at the quayside, the gangway of the five o'clock ferry was about to be raised. Govern rushed forward brandishing his warrant card and he and Beck were allowed to jump on. High above them, the passengers stared down, momentarily diverted from the sight of the sailors' preparations for departure. One man in particular was taking note of the arrival of the inspector and his sergeant. He turned back to his two daughters and beckoned to them to follow him.

As the boat eased away from the dock and began its slow journey across the Channel, Govern and Beck tried to find their quarry amongst the milling crowds now taking shelter below deck from the bitter February wind. Some were going one way in search of the cafeterias, others in the opposite direction making for the duty-free shops. Others still were making for the bar.

'Like looking for a needle in a haystack, sir!' Beck commented. Govern paused to glance at his watch. 'We've got another hour and twenty minutes to find them,' he said. 'They're here somewhere.'

Julian Matheson, with his daughters on either side of him,

was standing at the furthermost point in the bow of the boat. He was holding a bag of golf clubs by his side. The wind was blowing the girls' hair about their faces, which looked pinched and drawn. Sir Julian himself looked grave. He turned to look from one to the other.

'You've told me everything, haven't you?' he said. 'It's important I know *everything*. If this man Rivers really was about to rape you, Pops, Rose had every right to hit him. But if he was simply threatening to reveal some misdeed – one of you was pregnant or you'd been taking drugs or something, then I wouldn't be doing what I can to help you. Words of honour, both of you?'

They spoke in unison.

'Word of honour, Papa!'

'Right then!' he said and reached into his bag of clubs for Poppy's driver.

Five metres away, Beck and Inspector Govern appeared from beneath the bridge. They were just in time to see the twins' father swing the golf club backwards before hurling it with all his force into the darkness out to sea.

'There goes the evidence!' Beck murmured as Govern went forward to address Sir Julian.

'Disposing of evidence is a criminal offence, sir,' he said quietly.

Sir Julian showed no surprise at the men's arrival. His eyebrows lifted as he said: 'I suspect your intention is to arrest me, Inspector? Dare I hope that you are a man of integrity and that all you are really concerned with is that justice should be done? If you knew the facts—'

'Oh, I do, Sir Julian, I assure you – all the facts going back to last April when Mr Gordon Rivers died.'

Sir Julian was silent for a moment. Then he put an arm round each of the girls' shoulders. Still looking directly into Govern's eyes, he said quietly: 'There's a very special bond, you know, Inspector, between identical twins. Even if they are not together, one will know if the other is in trouble.'

He glanced briefly at his daughters. They were huddled together now, their ungloved hands entwined, their faces white and pinched with cold.

'Tell me, Inspector,' Sir Julian continued, 'if you thought your daughter was about to be raped? What would you do?'

Govern drew a deep breath.

'I suppose I'd do my best to protect her, sir, and if I accidentally killed the man in the process, well, I think I might come to the conclusion that justice had been done. But we are talking hypothetically, are we not? And by the way, sir, was that your daughter's golf club you just threw into the sea?'

Sir Julian nodded.

'Rose and Poppy were telling me that they never intended to use it again. It was my idea to jettison it. Dare I hope that you two gentlemen agree that I was morally justified in doing so?'

Beck followed Govern down to the welcome warmth of the bar, his face thoughtful.

'Are you really going to leave it like that, sir?' he asked.

Govern sighed.

'There's no evidence, David – that lies at the bottom of the English Channel. There's not even a written word to say *why* Barry Russell was blackmailing the girls, only Betty Russell's letter to me saying what she thought she'd overheard. Come to that, the P and R in Russell's account book could refer to a couple of chaps called Peter and Robert! Nor is Gordon Rivers going to pop up from his grave and say he tried to rape Poppy. Barry Russell isn't here to confess that he was blackmailing the twins. What purpose would there be in my arresting them? Only heartbreak for all of them and a huge and unnecessary cost for the country without any chance whatever of a conviction. Besides . . .'

'Besides what, sir?' Beck prompted as Govern paused.

'Cicero said – in Latin, mind you: "The strictest justice is often grossest injustice."'

Beck frowned.

'Not quite sure what that means, sir.'

Govern's smiled widened.

'Let's just say I wouldn't really want a conviction. You see, David, although I shouldn't be saying this, I tend to agree with Matheson that, bearing in mind all those girls must have been through in the last ten months, justice has already been done.'

Seventeen

May

John McNaught
Flat 2
Station Road
Ferrybridge

Dearest Rose,

I was going to email you, but on second thoughts I realized you might not want some of the details of this letter open to public scrutiny – i.e. anyone else who uses your computer. I have managed – not without some difficulty it has to be said – to obtain your address in France from the bursar, who was disinclined to reveal it. Had you left instructions that he was not to do so, I ask myself? It doesn't matter – I have it and I can now write and tell you I love you and that I am hoping like hell that you still have some love left for me.

Rose, darling, I now know everything that happened that dreadful night last April when you rushed out of the club. I can imagine the look on your face as you read this but if anyone is to blame it's me for not going with you. Then I, not you, would have been the one to deal with Rivers. No matter now – it's all in the past, and what does matter is that I'm crazy about you and want you to marry me.

When you and Poppy quit England that day with your father without even saying goodbye, Fred and I came to the conclusion that, after a wonderful start to our relationships,

181

you both became bored and were only hanging on until
something – someone – better turned up! Fred's okay now.
He's dating a girl who lives near him in Glasgow. I, however,
have never stopped loving you, Rose. I did try. This Easter
recess I met with a really zingy American girl – but she wasn't
you, Rose, and I realized it was only you I wanted.

I imagine you are wondering – not without some trepida-
tion – how I came to know what happened. You'll be as dumb-
struck as I was at the extraordinary chain of disasters Rivers
set in motion that awful night. Of all people, you need to know,
so here goes.

Yesterday I was playing golf with David Beck and we came
to the 5th hole. We were waiting to play when, for no particular reason, I mentioned how you and Poppy had a 'thing' about
the 5th. That's when David – God bless him – told me the
facts, in strictest confidence I should say, as he's not supposed
to talk about the events.

They came to light through a bizarre happening – a break-
down of the relationship between Miss Cahill and Kevin Harris.
As you know he was totally under the thumb of that Spanish
prima donna of a wife of his and, after a whole lot of nagging,
he'd agreed to put Cheyne Manor estate up for sale. The first
poor old Cahill got to know about it was when he gave her a
month's notice; said his wife had insisted they get someone
younger who'd attract the guys; that he'd give her a good
reference, etc.

Well, you can imagine how the poor old dear felt – cast on
the dump at an age when she hadn't a hope of getting another
similar job. It seems she actually loved Harris – only love of
her life and so on. Well, that old adage about there being
nothing as deadly as a woman scorned – when she'd got over
her shock, she decided to make certain the wife would never
be able to enjoy her life with the man *she* wanted. So she
shopped Harris – well and truly.

Rose, darling, it was she who found Rivers' body in the
bushes. She realized at once there had been a murder and told
Harris. To avoid any unpleasant publicity they put Rivers'

body in Harris's car and drove him to the hospital. The old girl then said she'd found Rivers on Manor Drive. David told me they had always had their suspicions about that but could neither prove nor disprove it.

After Miss Cahill's confession, the inspector put two and two together. He knew from papers he found after Barry Russell's death that he had not only been blackmailing the guy who bumped him off, Jason Armitage, who, by the way, confessed to the murder, but you and Poppy, too. It was on record that someone had seen Rivers leaving the clubhouse on foot the night of the party and that a woman had been in the cloakroom five minutes earlier and seen Poppy limping and taking a driver out of her golf bag to use as a crutch.

So then Govern and David hurried down to the hotel to arrest you both on suspicion of murder only to find you'd just left with your father. As you know, they managed to board the same ferry as yours and saw your father fling Poppy's driver into the sea. Govern said it was the only bit of evidence that might have proved you were guilty; that now there was no chance they'd ever get a conviction and therefore there was no point in arresting you. He even went so far as to admit that if he had come upon *his* daughter being raped, he'd have done the same thing. So he concluded that, in a way, justice had been done. And I believe that, too.

Has anyone written to tell you that Miss Cahill and Mr Harris were given community service instead of prison? They were heavily fined for wasting police time. Harris' wife is divorcing him and rumour has it she's intending to clean him out. The last I heard was that he only has enough money left to buy a small guest house in Torquay. Believe it or not, in spite of the grief he has caused his ever-loving PA, she has said she will go with him!

And that, dearest Rose, is all the news, I think, although you might like to know that David told me he and Govern speculated as to whether there was any way it might have been proven which one of you used the club to protect the other. They never reached a conclusion and nor have I, Rose. I suspect it might have been you but even if it was it doesn't alter the way I feel about you. All I care about is that you might still love me a little because I want you to marry me – come out to the States with me when I go back this summer.

Of course, Poppy would come with us. Oh, Rose, my darling English rose, go to your computer and email me. One word will do – so long as that one word is 'Yes!'

Rose handed the letter to Poppy. A few minutes later, Poppy handed it back to her twin.

'Do you realize, if it hadn't been for Deborah Cahill, we—'

'Don't say it, Pops!' Rose interrupted. 'It's hard to imagine that poor woman feeling so passionate about Mr Harris that she was willing to shop him when he ditched her. He ought not to have sacked her like that.'

'Well, he got his comeuppance, as Granny used to call it, now his wife has dumped him. Rose . . .' she pointed to John's letter, '. . . you've been pining for him ever since we left England. You do still love him, don't you? And he really did . . . does . . . love you. What are you going to say to him? Will you marry him?'

Rose smiled.

'What do you think, Pops!' she said.